FRIENDS OF FOES

Rae Maree

Friends

of

Foes

By: Rae Maree

Chapter 1

No Matter What

"I don't know why I let y'all drag me out to-night," Cadence called to her friends standing in front of her. Her arms were folded snugly to her chest to keep the draft out of her plunging neckline. "Relax!" Lakenya responded with a wave of her hand and without turning around. "We are here for the free drinks I'm gonna get us and the free breakfast I'm always offered. You should ask your friend why we're standing in this long ass line." Lakenya bopped to the bass coming through the brick walls. "Kenya, Hassan is the DJ, not the club owner," Tahiry answered her directly. "You should have dressed warmer." She snickered "or taken less time slapping on that fishnet of a dress." All but Lakenya laughed. "Forget this." Lakenya grabbed Tahiry's hand, who grabbed their friend Jewel, who then grabbed Cadence.

"Just.... Blaze" Lakenya flirtingly called the bouncer's name. He looked up when his name was called, but a worried look came as soon as he saw her coming. "Lakenya." He spoke through his teeth. "You're looking good tonight." She said with a huge smile and attempted to place her hand on his thin shoulder. He swiftly took his hand and swept her hand away before he took his perfectly landscaped locks and tossed them over his shoulder. "Thank you." He said dryly. "Ladies." He made eye contact with Cadence and put some life into his voice. "How are y'all?" "Good," Cadence blurted out when she was pushed to speak up. "Just a lit-tle cold." She ran her hands over her arms and bounced for show. "we're all cold.", said the lady that was in front of the line before they walked up. "oh, we don't care." Lakenya laughed without looking at the lady. She knew words would not be thrown her way because her friend's reputations preceded them, and no one wanted those problems. Cadence turned around to get a glance at the woman Lakenya disrespected, she turned around and hung her head. "Well, since I know Hassan is looking for you, I'm gonna go ahead and let y'all in." Jus Blaze said loud enough for the line to hear and then stepped aside.

"Sidebar," Cadence called before they fully entered the club. The four of them were nestled in a small opening fit for a quick duck off. "I don't know if y'all were paying attention, but the woman behind us was Bugsy's wife." Three of them eyed Lakenya. "Not tonight, Kenya." Cadence continued. "I don't care how good he looks. You see what all of you me had put on tonight?" Cadence took her hand to the top of her bare shoulder and outlined her perfectly perky body to show off the sexy white pencil dress she wore. "Yeah, we know it's Gucci," Lakenya rudely spoke. "I was gonna say that I look too damn good to fight but… tonight. AND it's Gucci." Cadence rolled her eyes. "Well, I agree." Tahiry jumped in before the back and forth started. "We don't want any drama tonight Kenya. My man is behind the turntables, and I don't want to embarrass him." "Just stay away from the woman's husband," Jewel said her piece before she led them inside with a sway in her hips. The fire red dress glued to her body commanded the eyes of all. "no fighting." Said Cadence one last time.

"Cain would have a fit if he knew I was in here." Said Cadence before she downed the shot of tequila Lakenya passed to her. "He'll be alright, as much dirt as he has done, he should not be able to say a word to you," Jewel responded. "So, I guess this means you are back on now.?" Lakenya asked. "Hey, ladies!" A familiar voice interrupted them from behind. "Y'all next drinks are on me." He smiled to flash the diamonds in his gold grill." I didn't think I would see you all in a club ever again after last time." He laughed. "What happened, Boogie?", his sidekick asked. "Well, little Ms. Kenya over here was Poppin' her ass all over Bugsy while his wife was in the club. She almost walked the dog on Lakenya, but she got the dog walked on her by these three, you see here." He laughed heartily and shook his head. "They were banned from the club." He signaled the bartender to bring another round of drinks. "well, it wasn't this club chicken," Jewell clarified before they all laughed. The intro to Trick Daddy's "tonight" began, and heat turned up instantly. It served as a musical bat sign for Tahiry to hit the floor. She pulled a blunt from her bralette and lit up before she took another shot of Cuervo. "Forget Cain tonight and just have some fun." Tahiry winked at her friend while pulling her to the dance floor.

"Make way for the sexiest lady in the room," Hassan announced in the mic. Like an old school dance, the crowd stopped their grinding and formed a circle around the lady in red, and her sexy friend in white. "Her friend is alright, too, y'all." He laughed playfully. Tahiry ran her fingers through her long flowing, blown-out hair and closed her eyes for two seconds. She mouthed the words, ground her body against Cadence, and blew puffs of smoke with the eyes of everyone on them. Few cheers and hollers rose over the music, Hassan commentated the dance he knew was for him. Cadence was given a moment to shine though she knew not to overdo it, she still made a few fans of her own that night.

Back at the bar, Lakenya almost had her fill. Boogie had intentions of being the one she would have breakfast with, so he held his position after his sidekick wandered off. Lakenya had plans of her own. Bugsy was her weakness as she was his just as well. They eyed each other all night while Boogie foolishly fawned over her. Even when Bugsy's wife attempted to take his attention by dancing close to him, he wouldn't keep his eyes off Lakenya. Despite the warnings, Lakenya was determined to start trouble. Gucci mane's "freaky girl" blasted through the speakers, Lakenya left Boogie at the bar and disappeared on the dance floor.

Jewel kept close; she was almost drunk but lucid enough to pay attention. It was inevitable, trouble for the four of them. Cadence did not realize Bugsy's wife had friends with her this time, but Jewel caught it. Lakenya was feeling herself too much. Straight in Bugsy's eyesight, Lakenya pulled a well-known enemy of his to throw her body against, and it was messy, Bugsy's wife moved closer when she saw the steam coming from her husband's ear. Cadence and Tahiry found their way to the last spot of enjoyment they would have for the night. The crowd looked like it had swollen since they came in, but their eyes found their girls, and as if they were her bodyguards, the girls monitored Lakenya's troublesome actions. Bugsy kept his cool until Lakenya let her dance partner put his hands on her. He got a few squeezes in before he was knocked to the floor by a force he did not see coming.

All hell broke loose again. Bugsy's wife immediately went for Kenya but was stopped by Tahiry with a fist to the jaw. As usual, Lakenya froze while Jewel and Cadence fought off the friends of Bugsy's wife, who looked to have been knocked out on the floor. Pandemonium filled the atmosphere; security was blindly rushing people to get to the original trouble starters, camera phones were flashing and flying, hair was flung from one side of the club to the other, but the fight continued. Bugsy had his opponent's blood spraying from the stomping he was giving. Smaller clashes broke out around them, forcing mace to be sprayed. Tahiry and the girls escaped the chemical and fled to the car they drove together.

"Oh my God, that was crazy!" Cadence yelled as Jewel sped off. Ahmad told me no fighting tonight." Jewel yelled in response. "I told you all, no fighting tonight." Cadence replied. "Go to my house. Jewel cannot go home like this; her shit is ripped." Cadence instructed from the passenger seat.

Into her walk-in closet, Cadence led the pack. "look to your left and pick from the black side. We are not here to browse for our next night out." She giggled. "Kenya, you know where your section is." All the girls except Lakenya, who was wider and pleasantly plumper, wore the same size. Each of their phones rang back to back while they slipped on black jeans, sweatpants, and hoodies they pulled from Cadence's closet. "Hey, babe!" Jewel was the first to answer. "Oh my God, Hassan called you already?" She sucked her teeth. "yeah, we are alright, at Cadence's house getting changed. Have you talked to your mom? The kids, alright?" She brushed her hair into a ponytail. "Well, meet us at waffle house. I'm sure Hassan will show. Ok, love you." She hung up. Cadence put her call on speaker. "You out here fighting at clubs and shit?" Cain screamed into the phone. All the girls rolled their eyes while he went on about what he felt her business should be. "You lucky you ain't let a nigga get close to you in that white cause shots would have rung out. I saw your ass." "Yeah, while that bitch Monica was all over you, I saw your ass, Cain." Lakenya surprised them all with that news. "Whatever, I will see y'all at waffle house." He hung up.

"What the hell, Kenya, when were you gonna tell Cadence her man and his baby mama was booed up in the club?" Tahiry was answering her phone call with a text but stayed in their conversation. "I didn't have time to." Lakenya shrugged and squeezed into her hoodie. "Where you at?" Bugsy's raspy voice on Kenya's phone made them all cringe. "At my best friend's house. Where is your wife?" she asked sarcastically. "I think she went home to heal from the concussion your girl gave her." He chuckled. "Well, we will be hungry at the waffle house." She hung up.

Waffle house was full of the club patrons. It was the spot to hold and feed the night owls after a long night of drinking. An old music machine sat next to the door playing the same song over and doubled as a rest for the broken booth bench beside it. At a booth, their men saved for them; the ladies sat dressed in black like a gang of ninjas. They ignored the stares and points from around them and just buzzed about the events of the night. "Steak, eggs, and orange juice for the table behind us. Steaks well done, eggs scrambled, add salt and pepper, and make sure they are not runny." Hassan announced when the server approached the ladies. "what?" he asked when everyone looked at him. "Y'all has been ordering the same shit since high school."

"So, what's the meaning of all this fighting?" Jewel's husband, Ahmad, started the interrogation. "Oh, it was Lakenya," Hassan chimed in. "Everybody knows Bugsy doesn't play about his hoes." Hassan laughed and passed the humor to the table in front of them. "Of all the dudes in the club, Lakenya had to throw her ass on T-Bone. Everything was everything until he felt Lakenya up." He took a sip of juice. "Bugsy knocked T-Bone to the floor with one shot, then his wife went for Kenya." It sounds like a repeat of club Jumpers on Lakenya's birthday. I'm keeping Jewel in the house." Ahmad joked. "Well, I am sending Tahiry to your spot." Said Hassan, "And Cadence will be right behind them." Cain finally showed up. "Cain, you know you ain't got no business talking right now," Lakenya spoke up. "Shut up!" he replied. "Bugsy's on his way in, and you know he doesn't like mouthy hoes." He laughed.

"When y'all gonna let this scary catfight her battles?" Cain squeezed next to Cadence. "His wife is gonna get tired and bring a gun to the club one night." The other men agreed. "When one of us has trouble, we all do." Said Jewel. "And whichever one of us does not get shot; the rest will be ready to ride on the shooter," Tahiry added. "You know, three of you are mothers, two of you behave like you are, one of you is a wife, one of you are engaged, but you are ALL professional women. We are not in high school anymore." Hassan continued. "All that is true, but nothing has changed." Jewel stopped his lecture. "We are down for each other, no matter what. I'm going out for a cigarette."

Chapter 2

Just Like Old Times

"I went with a Moroccan theme this month." Cadence led the ladies to her massive den. "For once, can we do something normal? You are always on some bourgeoise shit, Cadence." Lakenya announced as the first to walk through. "As are you when you are around those clients of yours. You're just mad; my taste is finer than yours." Cadence greeted the other girls with a kiss. "It's gorgeous." Tahiry rolled her eyes. A blood-red tent with black and gold accents hung over the place, setting Cadence spent the better part of her day preparing. On the floor, a table runner surrounded by beds of plush pillows in a rainbow of colors. "I've been looking forward to this for weeks." Jewel plopped on her pile of pillows. "I'm surprised Ahmad let you out after last night's fiasco." Kenya joked. "Yeah, how did that happen?" Tahiry settled in. "He made Cadence sign a promissory note." They laughed at her sarcasm

Four servers came to the table after Cadence rang the small bell next to her place setting. Vegetable and beef samosas were the first Indian dish to the table. Noises of indulgence and content replaced the small chatter the ladies had before. Cadence drew the line at the Indian music that began to play. "Tahiry, you are first tonight." Cadence sipped red wine from her glass. "After much consideration, Hassan and I decided to have a wedding after all." "Yaaay!" Jewel and Cadence squealed. "You sure y'all can afford it?" Lakenya attempted to ruin the moment. "your man cuts hair and plays music at night. You're a teacher, and we ALL know you all don't make any money." She laughed. "my fiancé owns THREE barbershops and has four contracts with clubs that pay him top dollar whether the place is packed or bone dry. And this TEACHER will have her Ph.D. soon so cut the shit; we're doing well for ourselves." "well, that was uncalled for Kenya. We know

I'm pitching in as I did for Jewel's wedding." Cadence tried to diffuse the situation. "That's what maid of honors do. Soup ladies?" Cadence asked and rang her bell. "Cadence, you take the floor." Said Jewel. Each server returned with a different bowl of soup and an empty sample bowl for each lady. Cadence's Shrimp and coconut soup was the most aromatic; she knelt at the setting with her knees on her heels and poured a small amount of her soup in the sample bowls. "Well, nothing has changed with work. I'm still telling people what to do with their money and making damn good money doing it." She chuckled, "Speaking of which, I'm gonna wait until your men are around, but I have found the perfect investment for you guys. I will not go into it now, but just know I encourage you to take advantage of this. I am going to show you what it has done for my very first client. He's been with me for ten years and recently saw a major rise in his dividends after he allowed me to invest for him." She raised her glass. "aside from my salary, he blessed me with a huge tip, and California is calling my name." The ladies raised theirs to cheer. "well, you deserve it, sis, it's been a hard year for you." Tahiry smiled. "It's about to get harder." Cadence pushed her bowl of soup away and picked up her wine again. "Two of Cain's baby mamas are pregnant for him again." Cadence felt the heat that ran through her friends. "You are not serious?" Tahiry asked before pushing her bowl away too. "Um, Akbar!" Tahiry joked with the server. "Take your coworkers into the kitchen and hold off on the next course for a minute." "Well, I know it is not Monica since she was in the club last night," Jewel said with an attitude. "No." Cadence replied. Lakenya sat quietly in her place as if the information were not new to her. "He's gone for good." Tahiry clicked her lighter twice to spark the cone she stuffed before she came. "I packed the little shit he did have here, and I took them to Monica's house and changed my locks." A lonely tear slowly rolled down her flawless face. "Why would you do that?" Kenya asked. "He's your man."

"And everybody else's," Jewel interrupted. "was I the only one that noticed him say he saw Cadence in the club?" she took the cone from Tahiry. "All while rubbing his dick on his baby mama in the corner of the club." She blew the smoke and coughed a little. "It's about damn time you rid this nigga from your life." Jewel raised her glass, and the girls gave her a cutting look; they despised the word nigga. "I'm sorry I had to say it." Jewel continued, "He has cheated on you for thirteen years, had three babies which now will be five on you, done nothing but be disrespectful, I say sayonara bastard." Tahiry said, stood, and raised her glass. "Fuck him, his loss, her gain, no more baby mama drama, no more crying, and pain." Cadence stood to the post.

"Y'all know y'all are too wrong." Lakenya wouldn't agree. "Cain was there for you when you found out you were adopted." "So were we." Jewel scoffed. "He was there when you found your precious brothers and father." Kenya continued. "Riding in the back of the rental we paid for. "Tahiry cut in. "Good riddance, let's move on to you, Jewel. What's new?" "Nothing she beamed. Business is booming; my babies are healthy and getting stronger. Everything is how it's always been." "Well, I just bagged a big commission from a fellow real estate agent." Lakenya began her proud moments in the sun. "She's from Chicago." She refilled her glass with wine. "She was looking to retire, and her choices were between Greenville and Columbia. "Hmph! She lit a cigarette. "I showed her the five-bedroom four-bath in Mt. Pleasant. Y'all remember the one we said was perfect for entertaining." She went on, "Had his and hers everything, huge kitchen, master suite overlooking the lake." They all agreed. "She LOVED it! Then I showed her another five-bedroom two-bath, but this one is on Hilton Head Island. Oh my God, girls, it is GORGEOUS! I fell in love with the exterior. It's a two-story with a balcony, deck, and an enclosed porch with a hot tub/spa, and this one overlooks the harbor. Tahiry you would love it, the floors were carpet, stone, tile, and wood. It was just beautiful." "It sounds gorgeous." Said Tahiry and the girls agreed. "Well, my client couldn't decide, so she bought them both! The ladies celebrated. "That's not the best part." Lakenya continued. "My client wants me to come to Chicago and take over her business for a small investment fee, of course. "Wow! Congratulations!" Tahiry was the first to jump up to hug her friend. "Have you signed anything yet? Is it worth the investment?" Asked Cadence. "I didn't want to seem too anxious, so I told her to give me twenty-four hours." "Good!" said Cadence. "Tell her to give you a week. You need some time to research the numbers from her firm and compare them to yours. You should check out some of the properties, get a better feel for what you are getting into. Once you get the numbers together, I'll look them over to see if it is something you should be doing right now." Cadence finished. "I know y'all got my back." "I know you will be back for my wedding festivities." Said Tahiry. "Of course, I'll be here." Lakenya's eyes went up, and to the left, her smile was sly. "She means for the fittings, bachelorette party, bridal trip, rehearsal, and the dinner after," Cadence interjected. "Damn, that's a lot" "But nothing different from Jewel's wedding, and you will be here for everything!" Tahiry and Cadence clicked their glasses together. For the rest of the night, the ladies ate the rest of their delicious authentic Indian cuisine made from the Indian chef Cadence hired. From Tahiry's stash, they smoked and blew clouds into the high ceiling, laughed about their crazy lives and men until they no longer had the energy, just like old times.

Breakfast was a huge deal. Jewel, in the kitchen, working on grits, home fries, salmon with bacon and onion, oatmeal, homemade Belgium waffles, bagels, French toast, and biscuits, sausage, steak, bacon, fish and shrimp. A feast for her family she called it, their men were invited and did not hesitate to show before the food was finished. "It's been thirteen years, and we still have breakfast together after y'all little sleepovers." Ahmad chuckled and made himself at home at Cadence's table. "Yes, those waffle house breakfasts were everything until Cadence got her apartment." Everyone agreed. "Only ones missing are Cain and Tony." Said Lakenya snidely, then everyone went quiet. "No negative vibes this morning Kenya." "what? It is the truth. I could have invited Bugsy, but I didn't want Cadence to be the only one without a partner." She giggled. "I stand alone, just fine, thanks." Cadence replied and sipped from her coffee mug., "you've been doing it long enough." Lakenya shot back. "Hassan!" Cadence ignored her friend to avoid the word brawl. "Good news about the wedding, bro." "Thank you, Cady, just please do not go overboard." He laughed, "you had poor Ahmad stressed out for his joint." He laughed and cut into his T-bone. "okay!" she excitedly pulled a wedding planner from the small drawer she had built into the head of her mahogany dining table.

"The date is set, we have a few ceremony and reception hopefuls, the bridal party is a no brainer, with Jewel the matron of honor, me the maid of honor and Kenya, the bridesmaid." "I think I want my cousin Loren to be a bridesmaid too. Oh, and Hassan's sister Bri." Tahiry cut her off, and Cadence recorded her words. "Hassan? The groomsmen?" she asked. He wiped his mouth and sipped the freshly squeezed pineapple orange juice. "well, Ahmad will be my best man, Cain, tony, your brother Johnny and my cousin Anthony will be the groomsmen." "ok," Cadence spoke as she wrote. "Fellas, if your emails have changed, I need those. I see your mother a lot, Hassan, so that I will get hers. The colors are set; food is no question." Cadence continued to read off her list.

Time slipped away while the old friends reminisced over Tahiry and Hassan's love story. They were all there for the moment the two laid eyes on each other; they watched Tahiry make Hassan chase her until she was ready for a boyfriend. The pair completed the circle of friends that would last longer than expected. "Well, we won't leave with the kitchen the way it is after you cooked all this food, J, and you gave up your kitchen Cadence. You ladies go and finish your wedding talk; we will clean up." As always, the men looked out for the ladies, catering to them anyway they could. "Cady!"

Hassan called Cadence to the side. "Cain wants you to know he doesn't think those babies are his." He spoke softly. "But there is a possibility, and I hate him for it. Did you see him in the club with Monica Friday night?" "yeah," he hung his head. "I told him to chill out Cady, but." "it is not you; he is a grown man San. I am completely done, and I am ok, ok?" He shook his head and hung it again. "Just like old times." She said. "What do you mean?" "how many times have you pulled me by the arm to the side to try to make things right for him?" "More than once." He said softly. "More than one hundred. I'm done San, go clean those dishes." She laughed.

Chapter 3

PRESENT DAY LIVES

Lakenya

"I'm live right now, celebrating my success with friends." Her camera phone briefly flashed the two male friends. One friend with an 843 tattoo on his neck weaseled his way on camera by kissing her neck from behind, the second with long thick well-maintained locks kissed her lips. "yeah, we are celebrating." he whispered then tongue kissed her. "Hell yeah," she giggled. Soft moans and slightly sweet porn at the sight of the men fondling her in public bought plenty of views to her live video. "On a double date with both my boyfriends." She smiled into the camera. "We are here, and we are live at Ruth Chris. Treating me to lunch for this great job I have done. I'm about to sign off on something big, then the three of us are going to do something special together." She giggled again, and the friends high fived behind her head." After the double sale she made, she was named the top agent in the state. Lakenya was on top of the world.

She and her friends disgusted the surrounding restaurant's patrons, with the three of them feeling each other, talking dirty, and practically having sex at the table. Lakenya turned the heat down when she spotted Hassan, Ahmad, and Cain following a hostess to a table near theirs. "Hey, y'all," she made sure they saw her after she saw them trying to avoid her." "What's up, Kenya?" Hassan said with irritation. "we saw your live. The girls are trying to reach out." "I saw their comments," she said snidely "I'll call them tomorrow." She kissed the tattooed guy. "We got to find you a man Ken." Said Ahmad. "Every time we turn around, you with a married man or a new clown. Now you got two." The boys stood up; the men stepped forward. "No boys, these are my brothers. We don't fuck with them." Slowly the boys slid back into their seats. The men shook their heads, laughed, and walked away. "They'll be alright. Just overprotective." She said to the boys while her eyes followed the men.

"Ms. Summers, I am thoroughly impressed with your record, and I must say you are well deserving of that award." Lakenya's new client sat across her cherrywood desk with a glass of champagne. "Thank you! I'm thinking of money green for the billboard picture." She stood to open the blinds behind her. "Green is my favorite, so I work hard for it." She said proudly at her desk in her olive-green Prada skirt suit, pink heels, lipstick, and pink framed glasses. "I see you play even harder." Ms. Charles sipped. "I realize your social media is super private; you have no pictures of yourself; your name is something no one would ever suspect." She picked up a picture of Lakenya and her friends. "Just know that I found it in time to see that live." She chuckled, Lakenya did not. "I know you see my degree hanging behind my head. This office? Belongs to me. It is decorated very nicely, right? Mrs. Charles took a second to look around and admire the original art from well-known African American artists, the expensive rugs and furniture placed throughout the office. "The smaller businesses you passed before you reached my corridor?" Lakenya got her attention back. "Pay me to do their business here. Anyone who would judge my work by my lifestyle and choose not to do business with me will take a loss." Lakenya finally smiled. "Is this a nonsmoking building?" Mrs. Charles asked. "There's a balcony right outside that bathroom for smoking purposes." Lakenya pointed to the double wooden doors to her right. "Mrs. Charles stood about six feet tall in her gold stilettos, her black Michael Kors pantsuit and gold accessories were perfectly set on her. She motioned for Lakenya to follow. Through the small spa bathroom, they went to get to the balcony. "So, what do you think of the contract?" Mrs. Charles lit her cigarette. "I have questions." "I'm all ears." "First, why are you trying to conduct business with this small-time country girl? I know nothing about the city." "Well first, you have risen above all agents in the state of South Carolina, why would I not want you? You remind me of young me, and you have the potential to lead Illinois as well. I'm well connected, city officials, celebrities, CEOs, the well off's and even the hustlers come to me." She pulled her cigarette. "Twenty years is enough for me; I'm ready to settle down and pay full attention to my man." She shrugged. "I didn't see a portfolio of your clients or any property listings." Lakenya's curiosity was peaked. "I want to invite you to look around for yourself. I do not deal with the computers and paperwork, and I gave my assistant the week off when I came here. Flight, hotel accommodations, food, everything is on me. Email me your flight dates, and your ticket will be booked immediately." She crushed her cigarette butt and let herself out.

Tahiry

"Babe, it's been a while since we've been able to do this." Hassan pointed to the candles and wine on the table, along with his favorite steak dinner. "We've been working so much babe, I've missed you." She smiled. "Are we okay?" she asked in a childlike voice. "Always baby. I am glad we have this chance because I want to talk to you about some things." Tahiry shifted in her seat as if she knew what was coming. Hassan picked up his plate to move closer to her. "It's so quiet in here, Tahiry. I'm ready for some babies." He smiled and ate. Tahiry's appetite was gone. It was just as she thought, the baby talk again. "I think we should see a doctor." He suggested. "I've been giving you good loving forever; I mean, I know you were on birth control for a long time, but you got off when we got engaged, right?" "yes, baby," she spoke hesitantly. "How about I get one of those ovulation tests from the store, and we keep track that way first, then if nothing happens, we'll go to the doctor okay?" "Ok, baby, I'll go with you." He smiled. "Hey, I don't want to be pregnant at my wedding Hassan." "Okay, let's make a deal. We will use condoms until one month before the wedding. Everyone, but Cadence has kids, and you know I want them too." "Yes, Hassan." She sighed. "You know motherhood scares me." He put down his knife and fork. "You've mentioned it but never said why." "Well, you witnessed my upbringing, babe. I've always been good at taking care of me, but I don't know if I can selflessly take care of a baby." "I promise you are not alone, and you will not be in the future Tahiry. If we would have had kids when Kenya and Jewell started, we would still be where we are. We are each other's motivators; it may have been a little tougher but look at them. I just want babies. Whatever needs to be done must happen, okay?" "Okay, San." She said to rest his soul. "you're going to be a wonderful mother, babe. I realize how traumatizing your childhood was for you, but you are not your mother. I've been watching you all these years to recognize any signs, and I haven't seen one. He grabbed her hand. "I'll never leave your side TT, and I believe in you so much, there is no way you will fail." He puts his finger at the tip of her chin. "Now, bring your sexy ass here so I can show you how I am gonna get you pregnant in a few months." He lifted her from her chair.

It was the first time Tahiry felt disconnected from Hassan's touch. His loving was still so fantastic after all the years they have been together, his kisses were electric, the scent of him positively toxic, but her thoughts were ruining her drive. While Hassan ravaged the body that belonged to him, Tahiry thought about the baby he wanted so badly and things that she should have but haven't told her fiancé. She was so distant; she did not realize he stopped because her participation was nonexistent Tahiry rolled to her side to stare off before she went to shower, not hearing a word Hassan spoke.

Jewel

"The South Sista's establishment, owner Jewel Powell speaking." "Hello, Mrs. Powell." A deep voice greeted her. "Mr. Powell, is that you?" "yes, ma'am. I'd love to see you for lunch." "Well, I'm here doing payroll for both restaurant and food truck, then I have a few evaluations left to complete. What are you hungry for?" "You, but I'll take a pizza." He chuckled. "Ok, baby, I know what you like, so bring your handsome self here." She hung up.

One grilled chicken with pepperoni and one supreme pan pizza along with Cajun hot wings waited on the desk for Ahmad. Jewel worked on paying her employees; she took a slice of each, with a couple of pieces of chicken after time was cooling the food. Her head had become too consumed in the numbers to notice night had fallen, and Ahmad never showed up. "Boss! Her newest general manager, Demetrius, appeared in her doorway. "Inspection is completed, I've received the emails from all the other managers, and everything is locked down. "Oh, wow," she finally looked up from her computer. "The day has gone. Take this home to your family. I only had a slice out of each." She pointed to the cold pizza. "Ah, it's just me at the house." He said sadly. "well, still dinner for a night or two. I know you get tired of our food." She shut the computer down before placing her glasses on her desk. "well, I never get tired of your food, but thanks for the pizza." She did not catch the look he gave her. "you're welcome! Well, my mother in law's church will be enjoying my cooking tonight. I'm taking the truck over there." "ok," Demetrius replied, "I smelled the oxtails and peas and rice back in the smaller kitchen." "Yeah, there's macaroni, cabbage yams back there too." She headed for the door. "Well, do you need some help? I didn't see anyone prepping the truck." "well, my husband usually helps, but..." She checked her phone. "I haven't heard from him since this morning." "I am available." He said in a way she should have noticed. He followed her out, leaving the food on the desk.

Jewel was too busy to worry about Ahmad's disappearance; it had become too frequent. He always has a colorful explanation for why he was not around and unreachable, so she looked forward to what she would hear later. Demetrius was her hero; he prepped the food, plated it, and took the orders while she served and hosted. A refreshing conversation between the two during the wait calmed Jewel's overacting mind. She gave him more than she intended when she confided in him about her marital problems. For a twenty-five-year-old, his words made an amount of sense to her. Demetrius spilled a few of his details. He mentioned he was single for too long, in his opinion. Demetrius had two daughters he was raising on his own, and he was actively seeking love with an older woman. That fact went way over her head. She was focusing on the fact that he was a handsome young man, and there was a feeling she could not explain.

Cadence

"I just want to take a break and think about what else I want to do with my life." Cadence explained to her brother Phillip. They sat across from one another in Jewel's Columbia restaurant overlooking the lake. On the deck by the water, the cool breeze comforted them so, their conversation lasted an hour. Phillip expressed how pleased he was with Cain's exit from her life. They joked about the fights where Phillip almost hospitalized Cadence's boyfriend for being disrespectful. "He's gone for good," Cadence assured her brother. "He'll be around, of course, because we are in the same circle but not in my life." She sipped her passionfruit cocktail. "I'm thinking about selling my house. I want something bigger." "why?" Phillip asked. His server finally brought his seafood platter. "You don't have a husband or kids." He chuckled. "I'm preparing for them." She laughed. "You're leaving Charleston?" "The part I am in, yes. Kenya has a few places on Daniel Island I've been looking at." She dug into her loaded shrimp and broccoli baked potato. "I want to be rid of any memories, Cain, and I created. And I'm going car shopping as soon as I close on the house." "ok, sis, brand new everything." he shook his head "speaking of new things, I invited my homeboy to join us toward the end of dinner because I thought we would be drinking after." He laughed and popped a butterflied shrimp in his mouth. "we still can." Cadence fixed her eyes on the tall, dark and handsome dream headed their way. His flawless, bright smile reached the table before he did. "Cadence, this is my right hand, Frankie." Frankie, this is my sister, Cadence." "Pleasure to meet you, gorgeous." Frankie extended his hand. "Likewise," she flirted with her eyes.

He and Phillip exchanged a few words before he took his place at the table. Cadence gave him only a few seconds to settle before she asked what she wanted to know. "So, Frankie, what do you do for a living?" she adjusted herself in her chair." "I'm a partner in your brother's business." Cadence laughed. "I see." "our business," Frankie corrected himself. "what about yourself?" he leaned in. "I am a financial advisor. How many children do you have?" He and Phillip laughed. "Straight to the point." Frankie nodded. "Yes, one son, I am single, I live alone, I also rent out a few homes that I own. I am an only child. I'm a mama's boy; I'm a Gemini. I'm not cheap. I love traveling, the beach, cooking, movies, spending time with my son, and the lady to be in my life." "Thank you," they all laughed. "I'm a Gemini too, single, no children, I love the beach as well." Her cell chimed and interrupted. She checked and ignored it. "How old are you?" she continued. "thirty-five," he checked his phone next. "Have I passed the initial background check? May I take you to dinner?" Cadence sat up in her chair. "Are you ready to settle down? If you are anything like my brother here." "hey!" Phillip jumped in. "I've been behaving lately." "Yes, with the woman who sweeps me off my feet," said Frankie. "okay! I will go to dinner with you." She agreed. "Tomorrow, my place, I will cook." He winked.

"Cain never took me on a date." Cadence thought to herself as she examined herself at the full body mirror. Her beautifully bronzed body was stunning in the orange cocktail dress gifted by Tahiry. She slid into her red stilettos and accessories a before she pinned her hair up and left a few curls to dangle in her face. "Punctual," she said aloud when the doorbell rang, and she glanced the clock. Nervously, she walked through the long hall from her bedroom, calming herself with each step. Cadence smiled when she glanced him on her security monitor, holding a bouquet. "My God!" he blurted when she opened the door. "you are simply a gift to one's eyes." He presented the flowers then held his arm out. "I've never met a sweet thug before." She chuckled. "You probably never will." He replied and led her to his shining black Jaguar. He was a true gentleman. Her door was opened, and his hand was held out to help her in the seat. By the end of the hour-long ride to his home, they were laughing like old friends.

Inside the private gated community, Frankie slowly took the road that led to his beautiful cabin style home that rested on the edge of the lake. "Oh ...my...God. this is gorgeous!" Cadence could not contain her awe when the gate to his backyard opened. A massive flower garden that would shame Martha Stewart caught Cadence's eye first. Tulips, roses, sunflowers, and daisies lined the path to the boat deck. Frankie escorted her to his patio that looked the size of an apartment. Waiting for her was a rolling fire pit and a bottle of wine in a bucket of ice. "Your brother did this for me while I was on my way to pick you up." He softly released her hand when she sat comfortably on the lounge chairs that were built into the deck. "I can only imagine what the inside of your home looks like. This is so beautiful." She took the glass of wine he poured for her. "Don't worry; you're gonna get the tour." He sipped from his glass. "Maybe you'll be the one to add the woman's touch."

Chapter 4

Secrets

"I'm signing in an hour." Lakenya's voice was slightly raised to the phone on the speaker. Everything was perfect; I already have a few things lined up." She was moisturizing her face. "Congrats Kenya." Cadence cheered for her friend. "Thanks, girl." let the girls know what's going on, and I will see y'all in a couple of weeks." She hung up and continued painting her face with the charcoal mask. "That was fast." A deep voice echoed from the bathroom door. "I don't need Cadence asking too many questions." She washed her hand and began untwisting her hair. "Are you afraid of the questions or the answers you will have to give?" he asked. Lakenya scoffed before she turned to slide on the porcelain sink top. "come here." She commanded. As told, he walked straight between her legs. "On your knees." No protest; in seconds, he was where he knew she wanted him. Tongue kissing her lips and moaning as if he is enjoying his last meal. "I'm not worried about no questions or answers." She said through her moans. "I didn't want to hear her fuss about me going through with the deal without showing her the paperwork. We are grown." She said before she kissed the lips that just tasted her.

He slid into her with ease and whimpered at the feeling of her hot snug love box. "Tell me you love me." Kenya moaned. Her legs began shaking within seconds of his penetration, but she held in her cries of pleasure. "Fuck me hard and come quick." She snapped him into drive. "The pants and sighs from his lips to her ears made Kenya soaked them both. Mrs. Charles's name flashed across her phone underneath her thigh. Slyly, Lakenya turned on the phone and began the performance of her lifetime. She moaned and screamed at the top of her lungs and told her partner how much she loved him until her patience wore thin. She commanded him to come again, and he did in an instant. Are you afraid of any questions or their answers?" Lakenya turned her shower on. "We are in Chicago. Nothing could happen even if we did give the answers." Lakenya peeled the mask from her face before she stepped into the glass shower. "You are mighty quiet out there." She called to her partner. "I ain't scared of anything." He stepped in and pulled her by the waist. "but you know that." He slid inside her again and took charge this time. "you know that mouthy shit doesn't work with me. He pulled her hair and stroked her so hard she could only respond with a loud moan. "So, keep that shit to a minimum." He spanked her, and she moaned loudly again. Ten minutes later, she was drying him from head to toe and promising to watch her mouth more. That promise was a big one she knew she could not keep.

"My name is Lakenya Martin, and as you know, I am taking over for Mrs. Charles." She stood in front of the twenty-member staff employed by Mrs. Charles. "I've read a file on each of you, and I am going to spend the next two days doing my own little interviews with you because I don't need you all." Lakenya began to pace. "Fewer people mean more money." She shrugged, "I'll be downsizing to ten people. One of you ten will be what I like to call the overseer. I am from South Carolina; I have my firm and a sixteen-year-old son that I plan to maintain while my business here thrives, so the overseer will be the one making it happen here. "I'm tough when it comes to working. If you cannot close on a house twenty-four hours after a showing, then I do not want you here. We will not linger or be held back because of an unsure client. Be knowledgeable, go above and beyond to make the client comfortable, be helpful, and they will not have a choice." She stopped and smiled. "Let us get to these interviews.

Mrs. Charles stood by while Kenya took over her employees. She sat on the couch in the corner of her office, watching the people she mentored break into cold sweats while they interviewed with Lakenya. She weighed in only when they left the room so that Lakenya could keep control.

Once day one of the interviews was over, Mrs. Charles surprised

Kenya with the keys to one of her homes in one of the most upscale neighborhoods of Chicago. The face of the urban villa and the "rich air" made Lakenya feel she never wanted to return home. "It's yours for however long you want it," Mrs. Charles opened the gate to the building her penthouse stood. It was a dream; six bedrooms, seven baths, eight thousand square feet with breathtaking views of the lake and the city. With the caption, "Bigger things! A whole bigger league." Lakenya posted to her social media page of the sun setting over the city. Her phone rang and brought her back to her feet. "What were you doing? What time are you coming back?" "Handling some business, I'll call you back in a minute Cain."

Tahiry

"I feel your distance." Hassan snuck up on Tahiry, sitting on the side of their king-sized bed. She jumped and hoped he did not see. "You are cheating?" he said softly with his head down. "no!" she jumped to her feet. "I love you, San, for so long, and you know that." "It's hard to tell right now." He slowly walked in. "I haven't kissed you in ten days; the last time we made love, you wouldn't look me in my eyes." He sighed. "it's because I know I'm not going to get pregnant San." "You don't know that." "yes, I do. I never stopped taking my birth control." She hung her head. Every second of silence scared her more than the one before. Hassan's short, shallow breaths were the only indication that he was still with her. "even after I asked you too?" he asked with disbelief, "even after I asked you to stop taking them?" he looked to her. Tahiry could only keep her head down and think about how she just hurt the love of her life. "I've never lied to you, never cheated." His voice cracked, and he began to rock at the edge of the bed. "I know," she whispered. "Do you know I never asked you for anything? Do you know you never had to work? Do you know how many women would jump at the chance to have my babies?" That question smacked her face. She did not argue because she felt she deserved that.

"I know you know I am thirty-five years old." He jumped up. Tahiry jumped at the thought of Hassan walking out on her.

Never had she ever been fearful of the hold she had on him would loosen. "I can't believe this shit." Hassan walked in their closet. "I proposed to you." He appeared at the door of the closet with a duffel bag in his hand. "Were you ever gonna tell me why we never had kids all this time? Even though I was begging you to have them." He began to pace angrily. Tahiry tried to answer, but he would not let her. He walked back into the closets and yelled out, "you were gonna control me forever." He laughed. "I did everything for you since the day I met you.

Tahiry could only sit on the edge of her bed in silence. Hassan continued to rant about his feelings of disrespect and stupidity. Her mind wavered to their younger days and how he spoke nothing but the truth. From the day they met, his only priority was to make her happy. "I don't mean to throw anything in your face; everything I did was for love." He said softly but loudly enough. "What else have you lied about?" he appeared again. Tahiry lied when she responded, "nothing, Hassan, I swear. You know my issue with this." "excuses," he interrupted. "we have talked about this." He stressed. "I'm done talking about it."

Tahiry's heart felt like it stopped. Her knees would not hold up, and her arms went numb. She felt the cold wooden floor beneath her, and her eyes were fixed on the ceiling. Hassan's voice echoed Tahiry's name in her left ear before she felt herself being lifted. Hassan's handsome, pecan brown face was evident in her eyes. His expression was more of concern that love, and it struck Tahiry's tear ducts. "It's okay." He whispered, "you're gonna be fine." He left her side to get her a glass of juice and a hot towel. "Do you want to skip dinner and stay in bed. He stacked pillows behind her back before he gave her the juice. Tahiry felt terrible; there he was taking care of her, when he should have left her on the floor. "no, I need to get out." She said softly. "yeah, I agree." He grabbed his keys and his duffel bag and threw them on the bed. In the bathroom, Tahiry heard him rummaging through the draws and placing things in his leather toiletry bag.

A full apology was on the tip of her tongue, an explanation that had more depth and was sure to make things worse, but the words would not come forth. From her bed, she sipped her juice and watched her love pack his things. He gave her chances to explain, but she remained silent, feeling as if she had no right to speak. "I'm going to drive my truck." He snapped her out of her trance. He grabbed his bag and keys again. "I'll go to the dinner Cadence is having for you, but I am going to stay at mama's for a while." "This dinner is for your engagement." Tahiry sobbed. "Are we still engaged?" she finally lifted her head. Hassan stood in the doorway, and his eyes were red and empty. "I'll be waiting outside to follow you to Cadence's house."

Jewel

"Ma Jane, thank you so much. I forgot about this event we had tonight." Jewel talked as she walked out of her mother in law's house. "oh, the children are welcomed any time, and so are you." She kept up to jewel's heels. "where is Ahmad?" she asked. "oh, he is meeting me there, ma. I don't have time to talk. I'm running late." Jewel rushed faster to her car.

"Damn, I didn't realize how much she can talk," Jewel said when she cranked up. Slowly she drove into traffic headed three miles to her destination. Niki Minaj's "Bed of lies" blasted through her speakers. She lit a blunt she rolled before she left home then sped a little. "Hey, girl! Tahiry's voice replaced the music. "What's up, T?" "Nothing much, what are you wearing to my dinner tomorrow?" "um, Ahmad, and I agreed to match blue. I have a new skirt and blazer I have been dying to wear." "I know it's going to be cute. Have you spoken to Cadence?" Tahiry asked. "huh?" Jewel asked. Her mind was on where she needed to be. "Have you spoken to Cadence? What's wrong with you?" Jewel hesitated to answer, the darkness in the country surrounded her, the trees danced with the wind. Her thoughts were off, including the road. "Nothing is wrong and no; I haven't spoken to cadence. "why?" "Kenya won't be here for dinner tomorrow. Cadence does not think she will be back at all." Jewel sucked her teeth. "it'll be fine if she doesn't. Do you have anyone in mind that could take her place? Cadence will need that name as soon as she hears this?" Tahiry laughed, "yeah, I want it to be as perfect as your wedding." Jewel laughed. "I am serious; everything was perfect; you guys are perfect. I hope Hassan and I can be half the couple you are." "Whoa T. I wouldn't say all of that." "you are so modest. You should teach a class." Tahiry laughed, "what kind of class?" Jewel asked. "marriage, relationships, love, sex." Tahiry replied. "sex?" Jewel laughed, "yes! You've been doing something extra special to keep that man all these years." "Hmph, you've kept Hassan girl stop." Jewel's eyes skimmed the street signs warning her turn soon. "Listen, I am going into the country. I'll see you at dinner tomorrow. "Jewel hung up before Tahiry could say goodbye.

Seconds later, Jewel's music was interrupted again, this time it was Cadence. "Hey, pretty girl," Jewel answered. "Hey, J! How are you?" "Good girl, on my way to an event we were invited to." "Okay, I haven't spoken to you for a few days. Everything okay? "yeah, the restaurants and the trucks have been busy, the kids haven't been feeling well since the weather change, and Ahmad has had issues with work. Ugh, it has been a mess." Cadence chuckled, "super J to the rescue, I know you are holding it down though, you always do." "I guess." Jewel came upon the road for her turn. She made the left on the longest road in the county. No streetlights, many old trees, older houses, bendy curves, and abandoned buildings were all along the stretch. "No guess Jewely, you have always held it down, you kept us in line, your life, family, and marriage are always together. You are our inspiration, girl." "What did you call me for Cadence?" Jewel dismissed her friend with a chuckle. "Well, I got my Audi today; I was calling to ask you to see if your baby sister still needs a car." "Yeah, she does. She is going to flip at the chance to buy your beamer?" No, she can have it. Tell her to go shopping with the money. I manage her money, so I know she can afford to." "oh, she is going to DIE," Jewel laughed. "How about we surprise her after school with it tomorrow?" "yes, we will do that, you should call Tahiry. I must go so I can focus on this road. See you tomorrow." She hung up

Finally, she was near her destination. Sixty miles per hour reduced to twenty-five. Jewel's heart sped up every second she slowed down. "Be cool," she said to herself. Into an empty yard, jewel made a right and immediately turned her lights and radio off. She stopped at the head of the driveway and said a quick prayer before letting herself out of her car. The house that stood before her looked decades-old but vintage beautiful. What looked like a million windows between both stories of the house were all blacked out except where one single candle burned downstairs. Jewel stood in place for twenty minutes staring at the old brick home. She began the stroll towards the house, dressed in all black with a hat to hold the head full of hair she proudly sported. "I guess he forgot." She said out loud and lit the other half of her blunt while continuing to walk. Her heart pounded harder; her mind raced faster than ever. At the foot of the steps, she paused to note no vehicles were in the yard, and the garage doors were closed. Jewel chuckled and started up the stairs. Her mind went blank, her body began to heat, and an evil smile came across her face. Just as she reached the top of the steep steps, a naked woman's silhouette flashed by the candle's light. Jewel quickly tossed the blunt then kicked the wooden door wide open. There Ahmad stood naked, the woman coming up from her knees. "I guess you forgot who the fuck I am," Jewel said in rage.

Cadence

"I'm proud of you." Phillip sat next to his sister on her new patio. "From the moment I met you, you have gone for and gotten everything you wanted, and that includes meeting me." Cadence laughed. "Thank you. I have no regrets." She playfully punched him. "How did it go with Frankie?" "Great! He's going to be my date for all the wedding events." She smiled. "he paid for my movers, and he bought and had the chandelier installed in my foyer. I hope he knows I don't expect Him to pay for things." "oh, he knows! He has an eye for fine things, and he was impressed with what you had." Cadence smiled. "Are you alright around here without Cain?" Phillip was vaguely familiar with her history with her ex. "Fine." Cadence smiled, "I have gotten rid of every memory of him, and I have not heard from him." Cadence could not hide her pain behind her smile, but her brother would not mention it. "well, even though you think an hour and a half drive is too long for a brother to drive for his blood, I will be here any time you need me. I'm dropping everything." "Thanks, Phil!" she grabbed his hand, "between you, my brothers Pj, bliss and the crew, my support system is phenomenal." She smiled. "Have you heard from mom?" he asked. "not since she needed that two thousand dollars." Cadence sighed. "What about your pop?" "He called for my birthday." She stared out at the sun setting behind the lake. "My adopted parents are still as active as always. I am still Flora's only girl.

"I'd like to know the story, though." "what story? "Phillip asked before he ate the chicken from the drumette in one bite. "The story of my conception, my birth, my adoption." Phillip nodded. "Why is our mother still married to your father? I, the middle child of six, the only one to be given up at birth." Cadence smirked. "My father has given me his side." Cadence licked some teriyaki sauce from her fingers. "Typical story, he didn't know mom was pregnant; he was just as shocked as me when we met." Phillip caught her staring off. "He's got a nice family. A lot like the one that raised me. My brother and sisters are sweet, we get along well, and my grandmother is the best of them all." She smiled warmly. "What is her side? Why won't she try to form a bond with me and not just my money?"

I will never forget hearing my dad say he saw you with your

adopted parents; he called them those people. He said he looked in your eyes and saw her." He sipped his wine. "I've never seen my mother cry before or after that." He shook his head. "I don't think ma will ever be in a position to tell you the truth about this." Phillip said frankly, "she is severely damaged." Cadence laughed "I saw the home she grew up in, I've met her siblings, mother, and some cousins." She stood up. "I've seen the home your father provided for you, your siblings and mother. Did your father forbid me from y'all lives? Her voice raised an octave. "I've heard stories of her upbringing, the silver spoon given at birth." Cadence laughed. "but she's damaged." "Accountability ain't her thing okay?"

Phillip snapped. "Just thinking about an admittance from her is a waste of time, Cady. One Thanksgiving, we couldn't get her to admit that she burned the pies, and she was the only one cooking." He shook his head. "She is a hard nut to crack sis." "Phillip checked his watch then stood to his feet. " If you choose to travel that road, I will ride with you, but just know, it will be bumpy, and the destination may not be what you are looking forward to.." he kissed her cheek. "I gotta go. My lady is meeting me at the gun range, and she hates when I am late." "Okay, I'll call you." Cadence smiled until he disappeared into her backdoor.

A heavy sighed filled the air after Cadence plopped back into her chair. Her eyes were fixed on the small drawer on the top of her kitchen island camouflaged in the same marble. Through the double glass doors, Cadence walked to the drawer and gently pulled it open. The contents inside were not anything she was proud of, hence her hesitation to dive her hand inside. Regardless, she did. Back on her patio, she sat on her favorite furniture piece and turned her cell phone off. Her favorite book, "Devil in the White Suit," sat face down on the table next to her. She placed it in her lap to lay down the knife she removed from the drawer. "So, this is what it's come to." She said to herself before she sprinkled the white powder on the face of the author then lifted some with the knife. She sniffed the substance then sat back with euphoria.

Chapter 5

Unbelievable

"Heey! Thank you for coming." Cadence stood at the entrance of the National Guard Armory, greeting the guests for Tahiry and Hassan's engagement dinner. She stood tall in her eight-inch yellow Louboutin's, her kindly fitted royal blue cocktail dress and yellow mini blazer. Mostly couples filed in first with loving smiles and clenching hands; the family came later and quickly filled in their designated seats. With open arms, Cadence welcomed them all before she took her place at the wedding party table.

The day had been perfect; the sun shined brighter than it had for a long time. Breakfast Jewel cooked earlier in the day was filling, no lines at the bank, traffic was light, and flowed smoothly. Cadence's hired make up, and hair teams, were prompt, and the decorator brought Cadence's vision to life. Frankie followed Cadence around all day, serving as her assistant. She was very flattered by him, his eagerness to help, and the interest he took in her life.

"You are glowing, Cady." Her adopted mother, Flora, stopped by the table on her way to be seated. "Thanks, mom." She half-smiled. "oh, I am serious." Flora knew the smile was not genuine. "Your skin is flawless. I saw you smiling, greeting the guests, and I said to myself how I had not seen that smile in so long. Is there finally someone new?" The photographer interrupted and asked to take their picture. With a small window of relief, the ladies posed for the photo with their arms intertwined. "Um, it's time to get started, mom." She kissed her cheek and dodged the question. Immediately she locked eyes with Frankie and the thought of having to introduce the two.

Twelve gorgeous royal blue curtains hung over the windows, two tall flower vases filled with yellow roses stood on each side of the enormous windows. Twenty-five round tables had been placed around the dance floor, each of them draped with a royal blue satin tablecloth. Submersible gold floral wedding centerpieces with floating candles and crystals wowed the guests. Twenty-five different framed pictures of Hassan and Tahiry personalized guest name cards, menu, and thank you cards rested on each plate. Smooth jazz music softly played while everyone mingled and found their way to their seats. "everything is so lovely, baby." Tahiry's mom Dana approached Cadence. "Thanks, mom" Cadence called her dearly. "Y'all are always doing wonderful things for each other." She hugged Cadence, "I tell my friends all the time, when she met you and the girls, she straightened up completely." Dana laughed. "together, you all had your share of trouble, but that was a step down from earlier behavior. I'm proud of her, proud of you all." Cadence walked her to the parent's tables "Um Cadence, have you noticed Tahiry behaving strangely?" they both looked for the couple. Instead of talking with guests together, Hassan and Tahiry were as far apart as possible.

"I know everyone can see the bags underneath my red eyes," Tahiry spoke to herself. She only became conscious about it when she went to hug Hassan's grandparents. The week leading up to the dinner was hectic enough, but the fight she had with her fiancé moments before they showed up pushed her over the edge. Tahiry made sure to dress like nothing was wrong; something her mother always taught her. She prided herself on being the best dressed of all the girls, and she still made sure Hassan out wore the fellas. "You are beautiful, as always." Grandma Edith kissed Tahiry's cheek. "Where is my grandson?" she looked around "oh, he is over there with his groomsmen snapping pictures." She flashed a full smile and pointed, and she kissed Grandpa Ben before leaving to speak to anyone else.

"you look lost!" Frankie stopped Tahiry. She laughed, "I feel lost. I did not know there would be so many people." She pretended to wipe sweat from her forehead. "Are you okay?" he asked, "oh yeah, um, just a little disagreement before we came is all." She wondered if he saw the tears forming. "I'm nervous, "she laughed it off. "oh well, this isn't the wedding." He laughed. Tahiry felt a sudden rush to tell Frankie the truth the whole truth she did not tell Hassan.

"I just want to thank everyone for coming tonight. Cadence stood in the middle of the floor with Jewel on her side, "can we have you all take your seats please we are ready to begin." Tahiry breathed a sigh of relief that the girls interrupted her confession to Frankie. "Take care of my sister," she said before she went to her seat. "I'm sure most of you know this young lady and myself." She pointed to Jewel. "for those of you that do not. I am the maid of honor, and one of Tahiry and Hassan's best friends, Cadence, and this is Matron of honor and another best friend Jewel. The fourth piece of our puzzle, Lakenya, and bridesmaid is not here tonight, but she sends her love. Once again, welcome, and thank you for coming to celebrate Hassan and Tahiry's engagement." Light applause followed. "We have known these two since we were twelve years old, we watched them get together, grow together, and now we will see them pledge the rest of their lives to each other. Cadence and Jewell took a glass of Champagne from the server she signaled. "We put together a small slide show to go back on their journey and take you all with us." Cadence smiled and lifted her flute.

A double-sided projector slowly descended from the ceiling, Marvin Gaye and Tami Terrell's "all I need "played at the start of the show. "Our very first picture together." Hassan smiled at the preteens posing like an adult couple on a slide. He slid closer to Tahiry and slid his arm around her. She melted in his arms and watched the slide on the I pad Cadence gave them when they got to their table. Tony Terry's "with you" blended into the end of the Marvin Gaye ballad. Images of the couple at school events, dances, each other's home, the beach, and the neighborhood park flashed the screen slowly, and those were just the adolescent phase of photos.

Hassan and Tahiry sat at their table, reminiscing over the times they recognized and laughed at the time they did not. A high school graduation picture of the two led off the second half of their relationship. Photos of him helping her move into her dorm room, she is posing with him at his barber school, the graduation, and on a ladder helping him hang the sign on his first shop. Everyone was in tears by the end of the slideshow. Hassan and Tahiry were so moved by the slideshow they had joined Jewell and Cadence on the floor behind Ahmad. As far as the eye could see, the future husband and wife team looked picture perfect. They were holding hands and sneaking kisses when they thought no one was watching. Before dinner was served, he looked lovingly into his fiancé's eyes and gave a heartfelt plea for her undying love, as if he were proposing all over again. Tahiry was relieved, she saw stars again when they locked eyes. Her heart found its steady pace, and the smile she displayed was finally real. Blinded by Hassan's respect for Cadence's hard work and money, Tahiry fell comfortably in the notion of having her man back.

"Surprise!!" Lakenya walked up behind the bridal party table. "well, did I miss the wedding? Cause this looks like the reception." She pointed around the decked-out room and laughed. "How did you get in here?" Cadence asked, "I had the doors locked before we started." "Girl, bye! So much for security when they are close to you. Those boys have been after me for years." She bragged and twerked a little. "Don't tell Troy." She put her finger to her lips. "Troy's here?" Hassan and Ahmad's heads turned quickly. "Yeah, over there talking to your parents San." They jumped up to go to their friend. "okaaaaay," Jewel sang. "Did Troy go with you to Chicago?" Cadence asked. "um no." she said quickly. "I'm hungry, where's the food?" Cadence signaled a server. "You're lucky we had a couple of no shows." "Let me guess, Tahiry's hating ass cousin Tia and her plus one. She had the servers add two chairs and place settings to the table.

Of course, Lakenya did not follow the color scheme of the night. Her apple red jumpsuit, silver shoes, and silver accessories clashed with everyone else's royal blue, gold or yellow. "Steak? Really?" Lakenya complained about the thick garlic butter sirloin sizzling on her plate. "If you were available to order, you would have gotten what you want." Tahiry got her together. "You should be happy you got in here, Kenya." She continued. "How was Chicago Ken?" Jewell asked to cut the heat down between the two. "Great!" Kenya dug into her food. "I'm leaving to go back tomorrow." "oh no ma'am," Cadence interrupted, "you have to get fitted for your dress, and since you cannot answer your phone or return calls, we chose a dress without you." Lakenya shrugged. "I'm not mad that you almost missed tonight, I am mad at the outfit you got on but now begins the events you cannot miss Ken." "Okay, three days is the longest I can stay." Lakenya reluctantly stated.

Hassan, Ahmad, and Troy were headed back to the table. "Hmm, so you and Troy working things out?" Jewell asked before they made it to the table. "uh uh girl. I'm just nice. I've finally convinced Bugsy to leave his wife, so I plan to stick to that." Lakenya bragged. Her carefree attitude about her relationship with Cain had been put on the back burner. "Ladies!" Troy said excitedly when they reached the table. They jumped up to see the brother they have not seen in months. "How have you been? Where have you been? Sit down; you look hungry." Cadence flooded him first. "I've been alright. Y'all know I went to help take care of my grandmother, and I am." He sat at the seat he was offered by the girls. "I wish this was Jewel's cooking." He smiled

"After I caught your girl in the bed with that small slime ball ass nigga Bugsy." Troy pointed to Lakenya with his knife. "I checked out for a minute." Really?" Lakenya dropped her fork. "We're gonna do this here?" she cleared her throat. "ok" she removed the glasses from her face. "Yes, I fucked Bugsy in the bed I bought for Troy and myself. It got a little too good, and I lost track of time." She said casually. "why would you do that?" Hassan jumped to the defense of his friend. Cain was usually the one to put Lakenya in her place, but since he was not around,

Hassan was always the one to fill in his shoes. "Because I can." She replied snidely. "Next question." She said smugly. "Why are you such a bitch, Kenya?" Everyone's head snapped his way because they knew he despised the word bitch. Lakenya's mouth gaped wide. "Because I can. Don't push me, Hassan. Next question." He stood in silence for minutes. Love songs chosen by Tahiry continued to play for the guests that were still eating and mingling. No one paid attention to the bridal table as they should have been. Tahiry and their friends could see a fire in Hassan's eyes, "who do you think you are Kenya?" he finally spoke. "I'm the bitch who took your bitch to the abortion clinic to get rid of your baby!" "Kenya!" Jewel tried to stop her. "Yeah, the bitch that sat with her in the doctor's office when the doctor told Tahiry that she could NEVER have kids because of the abortion she had." She laughed evilly, then sat back and popped a fried shrimp in her mouth to watch Hassan's breakdown.

Out of the corner of her eye, she could see Tahiry struggling to hold herself together, Tahiry's temper was the shortest of the four. Jewel and Cadence were in shock; they stood to the side, watching everything play out in slow motion. Hassan's hurt radiated to their circle, his massive desire for children was established on his eighteenth birthday when he blew his cake candles out. Hassan asked Tahiry to conceive but respected her decision not to. He stressed in front of them all that he wanted her to get pregnant after she graduated college. So quickly, those facts raced through his mind. "Let's wrap this dinner up, Cady," Hassan whispered. "I'm sorry to disappoint you, but this wedding is canceled, not postponed." He walked out without another word leaving them all speechless. "Boy, bye," Lakenya laughed.

For a second, Tahiry forgot where she was, and the promise to never put hands on each other that she and her friends made. Before she knew it, she cocked her hand back and slapped her friend to the floor. The music halted, gasps and stares came from every place in the room. "T! your colleagues are here, the president of the university you are about to be working for is here." Jewel was a little frightened by the glare in Tahiry's eyes. "We are not at the club, Tahiry. You cannot show these people that side of you." Jewel always tried to soothe her unmovable friend. Lakenya got up and sat in her seat, eating as if nothing happened. She finished her food on her own time, waving to the people as they left the venue. Tahiry had to be taken away.

"Why did you do that?" Cadence made it back to the table after the last guest left. Lakenya sat alone at the table, Ahmad and Troy and Frankie had long gone to follow Hassan. "Don't start with the questions, Cady." Lakenya warned her. "or what? bitch, I'll beat you in here because everyone is gone." Jewel jumped in. "Tahiry had that abortion right after high school. That shit was so long ago." "He was getting too high on his horse. Kinda like you right now, you ain't perfect." Lakenya snapped, "you just ruined Tahiry's life."

Chapter 6

In the Blink of an Eye

Well, you've cut your phone off completely, so I'll just say this here." Tahiry sighed. "I hate voicemail, but by any means necessary, right?" she chucked to herself and squirmed in her seat. On the side of the road, she sat alone talking into her phone. Darkness surrounded her, the familiar sounds of the country were loud but unnoticeable, one car had passed in the minutes she sat there. "I had an abortion." She confessed quickly. "it was the summer after high school graduation. I found out a week before I left for school, and I panicked." She began to cry. "I am so sorry; I love you." She laid her head on the steering wheel. A set of headlights stopped behind her and turned off quickly. Tahiry continued to pour her heart out. "Whatever I must do to fix this, I will do it. Just name it." Silence rushed her, and there was no wind, she had become speechless, the noises from the crickets stopped. She lifted her head from the wheel when she heard the rustle of leaves outside her cracked window. She fixed her eyes on the rearview mirror and saw nothing. Tahiry sniffled into the phone, still recording her. Hanging up for her meant she had to give up and let go, and she was not ready. "One last thing." She sighed. "I..." three hard knocks on her window startled her. Tahiry clicked the light on inside but still could not see until she put her window down. "Hey! What the hell...." Two bullets shattered her window and struck her in the arm and neck.

An hour passed; traffic began to thicken on the dark road that felt deserted just a few minutes earlier. Tahiry managed to keep herself calm enough to wrap her sweater around her neck wound that bled profusely. Her phone was out of her reach, panic began to consume her thoughts, in and out of consciousness she drifted, tears flowed and dried on her angelic face. "Hassan," she whispered. "I'm so sorry; I love you, please forgive me." The phone was still recording. She was too weak to utter another word; only take the many shallow breaths she was allowed. The faces of her best friends and the slideshow they put together for dinner played slowly through her mind until she lost consciousness.

"How are you feeling after tonight?" Asked Ahmad. Jewel kicked off her Royal blue Prada stilettos, then slid her skirt to her ankles. "I'm livid!" Jewell finally pulled the Chinese pins from her hair. "I don't know why we let Cadence convince us to make that promise." Ahmad followed her into the wide hallway lined with eccentric African art and family pictures. "Y'all weren't expecting to cross each other in that way. I looked at it more like you were saying no disrespect would be acceptable between you." Jewel sighed. "Lakenya always caused trouble." She scoffed. "hell, we got her out of a fight the first time we met." She walked to the room next door and peeked in on their ten-year-old son. "oh, let's not forget how annoyed I was with the questions about our perfect little lives." She scoffed again before she headed to the kitchen for a glass of wine.

"Babe!" Ahmad was on her heels "I know you hate frontin'" Jewell pulled a pack of cigarettes from the drawer she kept her corkscrew. The sliding of their glass patio doors was the response to Ahmad's comment. "you have barely said a word to me since…" Jewell put her hand up to stop him from talking. She sat in her chaise lounge and watched the birds in her backyard frolic together. Half of her cigarette and glass of wine was enough to make her give a real response. "your mom said to me tonight, "Jewelly, I wish your brother in law and his wife get their shit together like y'all. You make my boy so happy." I wanted to tell her what you did, but I couldn't ruin the night." "you do make me happy, babe. Please do not tell mama." He took a seat next to her. "She is going to know anyway; I want you to move out."

Ahmad sighed heavily. "That was the third woman I caught you with Ahmad. Not the same woman three times but three different women." Jewel calmly stated. sniffles from Ahmad filled in; Jewel did not look his way. "I was wrong, babe. I know we have been here before; I apologize." Jewel took a second to think about their history, she played herself a slideshow in her head, and it almost mirrored the one they did for their friends. True, she was Ahmad's first love from middle school, and he was hers, but never had she thought twice about being with another man. She thought about the nights Ahmad left her alone because of work, his dedication to the school, and his hustle in their early days. She stayed home, went to work, school, hung out with her girls from time to time, but her availability to him always came first. The last thought in her mind was the many men she turned away out of respect for Ahmad. "Your apology is not enough." She spoke tiredly, "You'll never know how it feels to feel unworthy of your mate." She lit another cigarette. "The pain of the love of your life choosing someone else over you." She blew smoke and exhaled hard. "Working so hard to be close to perfect as possible, not just as a lover but as the mother of your children, a partner, supporter." She laughed sarcastically. "Everyone knows you are married to me; it has been far too long, babe." Her voice saddened. "you know the word about me kicking in her door got around. It's so embarrassing. That was totally on me, but I am mad at you for it." She could tell he wanted to talk; she could see his squirm from the corner of her eye. "Maybe we have grown apart." She sighed. "I've got that three children meaty body; it's been seventeen years, I guess you should want different. I'm always so busy either with the kids or the businesses." "But you still make sure I have a hot dinner every night. Your body is banging, baby. I love your work ethic and your maternal instincts." He cut in. Jewel did not respond; she poured another glass of wine, closed her eyes, and let the wind kiss her face. "You're everything a real man deserves, baby. We haven't grown apart; I just messed up." After a few minutes of silence, her phone rang. "Please pack some things now, then come back when the kids and I are not here for whatever else you need." She grabbed her glass and left to answer her call in private.

....

Cadence's disappointment turned to tears. Lakenya exposing Tahiry was weighing heavy on her heart. With the cleaning crew around her busying themselves, she thought to herself the many issues Lakenya caused for others but said her blatantly spill on Tahiry was offensive. Tahiry fought on Lakenya's behalf too many times for Cadence to think of during that moment. Frankie caught her daydreaming and snapped her out with one of his everything kisses. Cain had become a distant memory thanks to Cadence's new man. It felt good to forget the madness that was a relationship between Cadence and Cain. An emotion she never experienced was drawn out by Frankie, and Cadence made no plans to let go.

She nestled into his arms while the crew worked their magic. They spoke in a whisper about the events of the evening and a possible solution to it all. Cadence was sure both her friends would never forgive Lakenya, she even suggested Jewel being the one to retaliate. As the peacemaker, Cadence began to make the calls to bring the girls back together. Without an answer from her friends, she took it as a needed break from each other for the night, but she refused not to hear from Tahiry. Cadence gave the four-person crew a hefty tip for their quick service.

In the driver's seat, Frankie pushed his Infiniti 2018 in the direction of Tahiry's hotel. Cadence sat on his side, redialing Tahiry. She felt horrible for the disruption and worried it destroyed their friendships. She was silent most of the way; it was not like Tahiry to ignore her call. Frankly, lovingly took Cadence's hand into his to soothe her a bit. It worked only a little, "I just hope she and Jewel haven't gotten together and done something stupid." She squeezed his hand. "Maybe she and Hassan are working it out," Frankie spoke sweetly. Cadence stopped in the middle of searching through her contacts to find Tahiry's mother's number. "Maybe," she cracked a smile and took a deep sigh. "God, please let my friends work it out, they love each other."

Frankie came to a sudden stop, "I love you, Cadence." He

surprised her with those words. His hand tightened around hers, and his eyes demanded contact. "You're not serious." She said in disbelief. "I mean, I know your feelings for me are strong, but I didn't know they were *THAT* strong." Frankie chuckled but smiled so widely and ran his fingers through his silky beard. "How do you feel, Cadence?" "um, why are we stopped like this, Frankie?" Cadence asked to deflect the question, she turned and looked up to see the line of cars in front of them. "Something has happened ahead." He said, standing outside the vehicle with one leg in the car and his hand on the wheel. "I see the fire truck up there." He got back inside. "Now, answer my question." He looked at her with his big brown mesmerizing eyes. "I love you *SO* much, Frankie." He was able to move an inch in the line.

"I know you do, Cadence. I can tell by the way you treat me by the way you hold me at night…. *AAAND* the respect you give." He kissed her lips softly. That tingle that melted Cadence every time she was around, Frankie stung hard in the moment. She lost herself in it and the look in his eyes that spoke nothing but love for her. "I planned to say this to you tonight at the dinner because I want everyone to know how I feel about you." The car behind them honked so he would drive the few feet that were allowed by the vehicle ahead. "They already know, baby, trust me, Ahmad, Hassan, and even Troy tonight had "the talk" with me." She giggled and rolled her eyes "The girls adore you." "I see you ran around me meeting your mother tonight." He laughed. "Hassan told me who she was." "we will save that for another time. Get back to how much you love me, though." He continued with his declaration of love for her while they inched their way closer to the reason for the backed-up traffic. They lovingly stared into each other eyes for minutes before Frankie came to his conclusion.

"I want you in my life forever." He reached into his coat pocket and pulled out a small blue velour box. "I've never met anyone as sweet, intelligent, caring, and sexy as you, and I refuse to let you go." He took his foot off the brake and put the car in park.

"Would you do me the honor of becoming my wife, Cadence Renee Parker?" He opened the box to display the biggest ring she had ever seen. "Is this real?" she joked to lighten the mood. "as real as our love, baby." They both laughed at his corny testament. "So, will you Cadence….be my wife?" "I would love nothing more." She took his hand before she accepted.

Traffic sped up suddenly, but Frankie instantly slowed to a stop. "Hey, isn't that Tahiry's car over there?" Neither of them paid attention to the blaring lights of the fire truck, ambulance, and police lights when they took off because of the excitement in the car. "Yes!" Cadence's smile faded with the scene in front of her. Tahiry's car was surrounded by first responders, and a crowd had formed behind their vehicles. Frankie could not stop Cadence from leaping from the vehicle toward the group. He threw the car in park and put on his hazard flashers before he went behind her. Frankie was amazed at Cadence ripping through the crowd like a football player. She was unstoppable. "Tahiry looks like she's sleeping," Cadence yelled out. The closer she got to the car, the harder both hearts began to beat; she was in fear of what she would see, Frankie, afraid of not being there to break her fall. "What the Fuck!" he heard her scream.

Out of nowhere, the sky fell, lightning struck the tree next to the passenger side of Tahiry's car, thunder boomed so fiercely it all put a stutter in their steps. The sight of Tahiry limp in the seat and the blood-soaked tan leather took Cadence's breath away. Frankie's yells and the horns of annoyed motorists sounded off in the distance. Cadence was stuck in place when he reached her. She should have been blinded by the rain which soaked her clothes and hair, but everything was so clear, Tahiry, who was so full of life hours ago, was now dying in front of her eyes. When she was finally able to let go of the wind inside of her, Cadence let out a wail that should have cracked the rest of Tahiry's windows. She fell to her knees before Frankie, and the police could get to her. "She's still alive!" Cadence's neck popped up when she heard the paramedic yell. She got back to her feet to spring forward toward her friend. Close enough to see Tahiry still, Cadence called out to her friend and cried when she did not answer. "Something is choking her. Something around her neck." She screamed, "It looks like she tried to stop the bleeding; it's a sweater." The paramedic shouted back. Harder the rain fell, but Cadence would not budge. She looked around to see the crowd of people gone, but their cars were not; they were watching on through the drench of rain.

After what seemed like an hour, Tahiry was pulled from her car. Cadence managed to reach the stretcher as Tahiry was being wheeled from the truck. She threw herself over Tahiry thinking emotional comfort she thought she was giving to her friend would help in some way. "Tahiry! Tahiry!" Cadence became irate when Frankie and the paramedic pulled her away; she fought them both hard until they were able to get her to the car. She would not speak, too distracted to make any calls. Frankie went through her phone to call everyone but hung up until he knew which hospital to tell them to go. He could only comfort his lady with his hand on her thigh while he followed the vehicle that took Tahiry away.

....

"So, what are you going to do, bro?" Ahmad asked the pacing Hassan. "I want to choke the life out of her." He grunted. "Who Tahiry or Lakenya?" "Tahiry, man. I don't have anything left for Kenya, dog." "Well, you can't, so what will you do?" Ahmad asked again. Troy sat by watching his friends walk around Hassan's childhood room. "I'm gonna get her cousin pregnant." Hassan griped, "She's been trying to give me the pussy forever." The men shook their heads. "wrong answer" said Troy. "Y'all have been rocking for eighteen years, you can not throw that away bro." he looked to his old friend. "Looks like I can." He plopped down on his bed. "So, I've been living a lie." He put his head in his hands. "All this time." He sniffled softly. "Bruh!" Ahmad put his hand on his friend's shoulder. "You need to talk to her. You know you love her; we know you love her, y'all just must work through this.

Don't do something we all know you will regret." Hassan's phone rang. "It's her." Said Ahmad. "Maybe you should give her a chance to explain. Hassan would not move. His friends continued to try to convince him to reconcile with Tahiry, but he was too stubborn to listen. He could only think of the many nights he bore his soul about the one achievement he was eager to get to, fatherhood. Tahiry promised him a team of kids and early retirement so they could spend most of their time raising them.

"Do y'all remember when I bought that pack after high school." Ahmad and Troy agreed. "yes, boy, you were the neighborhood dope man at eighteen." They laughed, "Remember how hard I hustled?" "And how cheap you were!" Troy cut in. "Eating pork and beans and rice every day," they got a good laugh out of Hassan with Troy's remark. "All to please, Tahiry." The smile didn't last long. "I also remember she didn't know anything about the hustling for a good two years." Ahmad pointed out. "That ain't the same; it was for her benefit not to hurt her."

"Do you think she intentionally hurt your bro?" Troy asked skeptically, "Not Tahiry; I refuse to believe that." Ahmad shook his head. "She may have been hard on you at times, but she loves the hell out of you, Hassan." Hassan stopped in front of his dresser and picked up a framed picture of him and Tahiry his mother kept in his old room. "She has some issues with being a mother because of her mother. y'all know some of the shit her mother put her through." "Well, can you blame her then?" Troy asked. "And you're mad at her for that?" "Nah," he set the picture face down and walked away, "she took away my decision to be with her or move on. She should have told me she could not have children at all. Here I was just the other day telling her I would go with her to see a doctor about it." He shook his head. "I busted my ass to make sure that woman didn't want for or need anything."

Tahiry's nickname in his phone "babe" came across his phone a few times before he switched it to vibrate. "She doesn't know that I have money set aside for our retirement. Believe it or not, I still have money from my hustling days. She doesn't know that the Ph.D. she's getting is just another accolade to hang in our new home before I take her around the world and get her pregnant in at least three countries before we come home." Hassan spoke sadly. "talk to her, Hassan," Ahmad encouraged; he saw her name still flashing across his screen. "Nah," Hassan said coldly, "I'm gonna get me a big booty bitch and treat her to the good life." Ahmad and Troy's phones started ringing like crazy.

....

"What's up? I'm catching the first flight back tonight. I have to tell you something, and it should be face to face." Lakenya, you are scaring me." Cain sounded worried. "I'll call you when I get to the airport." Lakenya hung up and pulled the shades over her eyes. A few people she knew were working at the airport, a couple she knew were catching flights. She dodged them all, which was odd of her accounting on how much she loved the attention. She went into a daze remembering her friend's faces after she spilled her friend's news. Lakenya knew the damage had been done, but she was unsure of the extent.

"A Thirty-year-old woman had been shot and left to die by the side of the road." Breaking news caught Lakenya's attention after two seconds of seating. An opening shot of Tahiry's car with police tape around it, investigators searching and medical personnel moving quickly. Lakenya looked around to see if anyone was watching, everyone was. The reporter depicted the scene and what he knew of Tahiry's condition so vividly, all airport employees stopped to listen. Lakenya pulled her earbuds from her ears and sank into her seat as if she were a celebrity trying not to be seen. "We have just got confirmation, the victim, thirty-year-old Tahiry Denise James." A cropped picture from her Facebook page flashed the screen. Lakenya recognized the background from Jewel's wedding. "Hey! Aren't you, Lakenya Martin?" Someone from their neighborhood stopped in front of her. "yeah," she said shortly. "Ain't that your best friend they're talking about?" Lakenya turned away from the screens. "Loading now flight 183 to Chicago, gate 12," the announcer said twice. "Her condition has still not been released, but a potential witness said it was pretty bad." The reporter's voice cut through before Lakenya hopped up and walked by the lady without acknowledging the question she asked.

"What's going on, Lakenya?" Cain asked in a frantic. She sat in the back of the uber, reluctant to answer. "Ahmad, Cadence, everybody's been calling me back to back, is my family okay?" "Yeah, your people are fine. I'll be home in thirty minutes." She hung up quickly and put her window down to take in the scents of the city. Nothing could take her mind off the situation back home. She ran intentionally and felt no remorse. Her flight was filled with thoughts of times she felt outcasted by her friends and how life seemed so much easier for them. Every man she put her eye on seemed to have eyes for them. Lakenya felt proud to be able to hang with them financially, but she knew that was the only area she could give them competition.

"I need a do not disturb sign for my door." She said to the hotel desk clerk. "I'm at the Meridian." She spoke into her cell. "Suite 1442, call me when you get here, you cannot come up otherwise, and don't forget my candy." She hung up, gave the clerk an eye then looked down at her luggage. Her bath was immediately drawn. Lakenya laid across the bed and puffed a joint she rolled to wait for her company. The tv played for noise purposes, a rerun of Martin sounded off with laughter. In time, the phone rang, and she was relieved she could finally turn her phone off, so she no longer had to see Cain's name across her phone screen. His name sat there with the number fifty next to it. "Thanks for coming." Lakenya slipped out of her dress and headed toward the heated tub holding her chamomile and honey bath. "What was Cain doing when you left the house?" "Stressing out. He said he had been getting a lot of calls from your hometown." Lakenya sighed, "would you just roll up, please? Then come get in the tub with me." She walked away.

Rascheen, an associate of Mrs. Charles, took the initiative of showing Lakenya the city when she arrived. He was too much of a man for her to not make a pass at soon he rows time, she invited him to dinner and made her move. The country girl in her made her irresistible to him. Before he knew it, his married ass was at her beck and call.

"So, what's going on?" Rascheen put his hands on Lakenya's soapy shoulders. "You seem extra mysterious tonight. Your man is at your house about to lose his mind. What's up?" he dried his hands to prepare her tray. He came back with a silver platter holding two Xanax, a joint and a glass of red wine. "You're gonna talk to me tonight, Kenya." He dropped the pills on her tongue and fed her the wine. "Go be with your wife. I'm not into you tonight." She said coldly.

Noon the next day, Lakenya went home to a nodding Cain in a chair he positioned in front of the door. She tried to tiptoe around him; he grabbed her arm so she would not. "Talk…. Now." He sounded angry. "Listen, I ain't Cadence." "You're not Cadence, but you know I don't play with you either. I haven't answered anyone's calls, and you said you would be here last night. What in the hell is going on?" he stood up and stretched, "Do I need to go home?" "no!" she yelled. "well, then what the hell is it?" he yelled louder. Tahiry got shot in the neck and shoulder last night." "well, then I do need to go home." He started to walk away. "I…" Cain stopped in his tracks. "You what?" he glared, "I…. don't think we should go together." He scoffed. "I could care less; I'm going to be with my sister."

Chapter 7

On the Brink

"She's been in surgery for six hours now; we haven't heard anything," Cadence spoke in a whisper to Tahiry's colleague. The waiting room was flooded off and on with family members, friends, and colleagues. Tahiry's mother and her pastor sat in the seats closest to the door for hours. Visitors and family members served them lunch, dinner, coffee, and whatever else they requested throughout the day.

Hassan sat in the middle of Jewel and Cadence with constant tears streaming over his stoic face. Ahmad paced the room, holding tears of his own, some of them from the thought of losing his wife. "I should have answered," Hassan whispered when his mother embraced him. She needed his strength at the moment because she wept as if she got news of Tahiry's death. He held her before helping her take a seat. Her cries were all everyone else needed to trigger the pain inside them. Into each other, they leaned for comfort.

"Tahiry James' family?" The tall, broad doctor who looked more like a football player came through the door with his surgical mask hanging on his left ear. He stood straight as an arrow with an unreadable stern look on his face. Everyone in the waiting room gave their attention to him. "They're all family." Tahiry's mother spoke to end the doctor's pause. "Okay," he cleared his throat. Hassan, Cadence, Jewel, Troy, and Ahmad stood together behind one of the women that watched them all grow up and considered them all her own. " Two bullets struck her, one in the shoulder which went straight through her. Now the second bullet hit her spinal cord." "no!" Tahiry's mother said shakily. She turned around and reached her hands out to Jewel, and Cadence then pulled them close. "There was some internal bleeding, and she lost a lot of blood as well." Everyone around them gasped in horror. "We were able to extract the bullet, but we will only know the damage if." he looked around and hesitated. "If what? Cadence asked, "If she comes out of the comatose state that she is in." A wave of cries went from the door to the furthest wall. Cadence and Jewel helped Mrs. James to her seat after she buckled at the knees. With no more news, the doctor left the room quietly. It was evident how immune to the scene he had become.

"Where is Kenya?" Mrs. James asked. Cadence shrugged her shoulders. "we haven't seen her since dinner. I've been trying to reach her, but I haven't gotten an answer." She rubbed her shoulders. "I've booked a room for you across the street. Get a list of clothes, toiletries, and other things you may need, and I'll go out to your house to get them. You should stay here or close by at all times." Cadence whispered. "Mama, James!" Cain appeared at the door. "Cain!" everyone except Cadence and Frankie said in unison, even Hassan perked up for a second. "Where have you been?" Tahiry's mom welcomed Cain with open arms. "My pops needed someone to help with the business for a while, but when I heard, I took the first plane home." He kissed her hand. "How is your father?" Mrs. James asked. "He's well, just had to do some laying off, so he needs someone to manage until he gets back to normal. How is Tahiry, though?" he slightly squeezed her hand. "good news, some bad." She whispered. "She is in a coma." She patted the top of his hand. "The police don't know anything." she sniffled. Tears formed in her eyes, she laid her head on his shoulder and rocked with him.

Cadence took the first shift of sitting with Tahiry. Right away, she printed pictures from her cell phone and framed them. She took roses and tulips from her garden to place around the room and brought music from one of Tahiry's playlists. "I'm here, sis." Cadence kissed Tahiry's forehead and tucked her into her favorite blanket from her and Hassan's house. "I've got a little decorating to do." She chuckled humorlessly. "Now, don't get too comfortable because you have to come home to us." She began to arrange everything. "As soon as you come back, you and Hassan are going to get married, and you are gonna do whatever you gotta do to give that man a baby." She slightly scolded. "Let's get some sun on your face." She opened the blinds, and the light illuminated her perfectly brown skin that was now clean from the blood that had dried on her face. Cadence glazed out of the window, down at a set of friends having lunch at her and her girl's favorite restaurant. "Do you remember when Jewell got her first job and brought us out to eat down there?" she giggled. "we were so broke, she almost bought one plate for us to share. The manager thought she was cute; he was plotting when we walked in., we ate well for free that day." She laughed and arranged some tulips in a vase.

"Cadence," Cain called from the door. She froze at the window and closed her eyes. "I came as soon as I heard." She still did not speak. "who is that dude I saw you with earlier?" she sighed heavily. "oh, my bad T." he walked to Tahiry's bedside. "Get well, sister." He whispered and took her hand. Cadence kept her place at the window, and she kept her calm. His disappearance was worse than a brutal breakup, and she was scorned. She wanted answers, a glass of wine, and an object to hit him with. "Well, I guess you won't be speaking to me." Cain paused for a second. "I can say what I need to. I am sorry for everything I ever put you through." She closed her eyes. "I don't know what I was thinking. We should have been the first ones to get married." That statement softened her up a bit, but she refused to show it.

"Good thing you didn't, huh babe?" Frankie walked through the door with Applebee's bags in his hands. "Hey, baby!" Cadence cheerfully turned around to greet her man. He set the bags down to get a good grip on his baby. "You hungry, baby?" "Starving." They went on as if Cain were not in the room until he cleared his throat. "Baby, that's Cain. Cain, this is my man Frankie." She ran her fingers through his beard, then kissed him. Cain walked out without a word. Cadence knew Tahiry would be proud of what just happened. She smiled and winked her friend's way. Cadence and her loving fiancé enjoyed a silent lunch together while keeping their eye on Tahiry. Cadence did not want to say the things on her mind that was worrisome, but Tahiry's condition consumed her thoughts. Frankie did what he did best, comfort Cadence, and soothe her with his words. He knew when to be silent, and when he spoke, he knew exactly what to say.

Hassan walked in with a duffel bag, an oversized Jordan sweatshirt under a leather jacket, and his earbuds connected to his phone in his pocket. He looked out of it, he embraced Cadence warmly and greeted Frankie with a handshake. He removed his earbuds and pulled another chair to Tahiry's side. "I just brought a few things, Hassan." Cadence looked around. "Flowers and these bamboo plants she loves so much." He looked up, "These pictures here." She pointed, "are for when she wakes up, no matter who is here when she does, we all will be around her." "Thanks, sis." Said Hassan in gloom. He sat back down to hold her hand.

………

Three weeks passed, with no progression on Tahiry's condition. It was the time of year where the weather should have been much colder, but everyone was still in summer attire. However, the more days Tahiry laid in the hospital, the colder the days became. Everyone held tight with the schedule; there was not a second that Tahiry was alone. Lakenya was finally due to show her face; her communication and concern throughout the weeks were not much to speak on, and she sounded hesitant when she called to say she would become. Tahiry was not her concern; her reputation was.

"You've become a city girl and forgot all about us." Lakenya's young friends had their hands all over her body. She laid naked in the middle of her king-sized bed lost in the feeling of Euphoria. "We've missed you." The dread head kissed her sweetly and palmed both of her breasts. "yes!" said the clean-cut sidekick after he took a breather from between her legs. "We should make her pay." Dread head laughed. "Nah, y'all should stay here with me." She moaned, "I have plenty of room for my addictions." She opened her eyes to the long silky dreads and the lips that owned them, closing in on her lips. He moaned with ecstasy when she swallowed his tongue. "Don't be greedy." Mr. Clean cut came up for air and sensually crawled over Lakenya's wanting body, "I've been missing those lips too." He glared into her eyes. Lakenya loved it, the attention she was able to demand from the two helpless little boys at once. During ventures such as those, she felt invigorated by the hours of desire her partners gave her. She often wished people who teased before belittling her in the past could see her in those positions.

It felt like airlifted her when they turned her over, Mr. clean-cut forced her hips in the air when he slid his head underneath. "ride his face babe." Sexy dread encouraged her while rubbing her ass. Slowly she rocked back and forth and sang a song of pleasure, and he let his tongue travel from the top of her neck to way below her hips. Two tongues at the same time made her forget herself. Her body jerked almost violently from the sensations. "I'm sliding in you." Mr. Clean bought his body up and whispered. "Oh my God, I missed you." She purred from the deep dive he took. Dread head's tongue stayed in place for a few minutes more before he occupied the second hole. He slid his fingers in and out of Lakenya's mouth, revving himself up for a pounding.

"Yo! What the fuck!" Troy flipped the lights on. Not one of them skipped a beat. "YOOOOO," he yelled. They jumped that time. "Troy! What are you doing here, when did you get to Chicago? I thought…." "Thought what?" he interrupted. Lakenya's addictions looked on while dressing. "Get these boys out of here, yo…" "Just leave y'all. You have my card, go get yourself a nice hotel." Troy slapped her to the floor. Dread head threw his clothes on the floor and lunged for Troy. The two of them threw a few punches before Lakenya broke it up with a gunshot to the ceiling. The boys scrambled to get their things and leaped out of the door.

"This is why we have problems!" Troy slammed the door behind the boys. "Why, Troy? Why?" Lakenya was tying a robe around her. "Because you introduced me to the life of loving two men at once." She smirked and lit a cigarette. She spoke of the threesome with a male acquaintance he asked for on his birthday. "I didn't come to Chicago for this. You hauled ass from South Carolina then demand I come to you." "you're here, aren't you?" she smiled. "You're pushing my buttons already." He shook his head.

Even though the gun was still in her hands, she froze in place, the tone he took with her was unpleasantly familiar. She hurriedly walked to her bedroom; Troy was close on her heels. "That walking away shit Kenya." His voice went up an octave. She sped up into her bedroom, then turned and waited for him. For some reason, he was a few seconds behind her. "Yo! What the fuck!" he exclaimed when he walked right into the gun. Lakenya laughed evilly. "yeah, nigga. Thought you were gonna put hands on me?" A cold draft fell in her bedroom. A more biting look came through her eyes, and she began to laugh. "Watch yourself, K," Troy warned. "NO NO" She took a step closer. "Let's go to this mirror, and you watch yourself." Troy backed up slowly toward the bathroom.

"Turn around!" she demanded him to face himself. "Do you remember the time we were in the drive-thru at burger king? Of course, you do. It was the first and last time we went there together." She scoffed. "we were paying for the food, and the boy at the window spoke to me." She said sweetly. Troy calmly listened to the familiar story. "When I spoke back, you slapped the shit out of me." Lakenya shook her head. "That wasn't enough, though. You blacked both of my eyes and broke my nose. I didn't go to school for two weeks." "Lakenya" Troy said calmly. "uh uh uh" she put the gun to his shoulder. "You are listening now." She aimed the gun at the back of his head. "Light me a cigarette." Troy slowly did what he was told. "That one beating led to years of physical abuse that no one knew about. Especially when you started that cocaine." She puffed the cigarette and kept the gun to his head. "You would beat me just for dinner being late." A lonely tear slid down her face. "The trick was to hit me where no one noticed. The girls wondered why I was not losing weight when I claimed to be working out, but I'm just walking around with broken ribs." "Yo, what you want? An apology?" he became agitated. "ummmm, no. I want you to feel some shit." She hit him in the back of the head so hard it knocked him out. Lakenya ran to get her cell phone then came back over him to finish her cigarette. 911 was on the screen, her finger on the call button. Troy slowly began to come around to Lakenya's screaming into her cell. She watched him adjust his eyes and rub the back of his head while she told the operator he was trying to rape her. Troy worked to scuffle to his feet, but he was still too dizzy. Lakenya gave an Oscar-winning performance until he finally got his balance. She quickly hung up the phone and shot him in the chest.

There was no panic; she never told the operator where she was, so she figured they would call back, or it would be a while before they arrived. She took his hand and scratched herself. Underneath her eye, she carved a deep scratch, she took both his hands and gripped her neck, leaving a print. She wasn't convinced. Blood needed to be shed, so she had made more scratches and broke the glass ashtray from the nightstand. Moments later, there was a knock at the door.

......

"you know the doctor has been talking to mama J about taking Tahiry off the respirator." Cadence and Jewell sat at their favorite little table in Panera bread. "She's giving it some thought." Cadence took a bite of her steak and arugula sandwich. "well, it has been almost a month, and there haven't been any improvements. Every day the probability of her waking up gets smaller." Jewel sipped her blood-red orange lemonade. "I don't care about probability and improvements, as long as there is a possibility, I will hold on to that," Cadence said with the stern. "I think mama J is just worried about Hassan and me helping with the medical bills." Cadence sighed. "You know there is no other way I would rather spend my money; she knows it too." "I know Cady, but you have also been providing room and board at an expensive hotel." "So, she and Tim could be close if something happens." "This has to be so exhausting,

Cadence." "But no different if it were you in that hospital room, or me or one of the fellas." Cadence snapped. "When she wakes up, we're going on a long vacation." Said Cadence with hope.

"Oh, my God! Troy's sister just tagged Lakenya's business page in a post on Facebook." Jewell read, "My brother was not trying to rape that bitch. The police better keep her because she's dead on these streets and the ones in Chicago if need be." "What the hell happened." Cadence picked up her phone to search her social media. "Troy is dead, Cady! Kenya killed him!" Cadence dropped her phone. "It says here; he was trying to rape her. Oh my God, this is crazy. Did you know he went to Chicago with Kenya?" Cadence's phone rang. It was Troy's sister Crystal. "Hey, boo, I know you've heard by now." Cadence put the phone on speaker. "Two seconds before you called Crys." "I heard your friend has been acting all kind of crazy." Crystal's voice was shaky and tolerant. "Yeah, she has been acting out a lot lately for some reason, but we haven't seen her since Tahiry's engagement dinner, which you attended," Cadence spoke carefully. "How is Tahiry?" "She is still the same. In a coma, still fighting." Cadence finally bit into her wild berry scone. "I'm sorry Cadence, tell Jewel I'm sorry too." Jewel heard but only shook her head; she knew what the call was all about. "If you see or speak to Lakenya." Crystal began to warn Cadence and Jewel without her knowledge. "Tell her out of respect for you two; I'd like to talk to her, see where her head is before I kill her." "We can't let you kill her, Crystal," Cadence spoke frankly with the protection of her friend, but the face Jewel made showed she did not agree. Crystal laughed sarcastically. "See you, ladies, later." She hung up. "She is not going to keep it simple, Cady." Jewell sighed. "Well, you know what it is." Cadence shrugged her shoulders. "Should we, though? After everything?" Cadence gave a few minutes before she answered. "Yes, Jewelly, what's up with you?" "I have too many other things to deal with than to get Kenya out of trouble…AGAIN."

"Well, what's up?" Cadence leaned in with concern. Jewel sighed. "I'm thinking of divorcing Ahmad. He's a cheater." "A cheater?"

Cadence asked surprised with a chuckle, but she smiled faded when she saw the hurt on her friend's face. "Yeah, Cady. He's been cheating for years now." She said sadly, "This was the last time for me. He's been staying at the house since Tahiry got shot, but I'm gonna ask him to leave tonight." "Why didn't you tell us?" "well, you see why with Kenya, but you and Tahiry always talked about how perfect of a couple we were. I didn't want to kill your dreams of a faithful marriage because it is possible." "I'm so sorry, Jewely. We wouldn't have judged you. After everything we've ever been through." "I know, I'm sorry." "his mother is devastated. She does not want this." "that's your mommy." They laughed. "Do you have to leave him?" "for now. Maybe a divorce will make him step away then come back a new man. If not, we will live separate lives." She said with finality. "Everything is falling apart. Cadence sniffled. "I didn't want to tell you this with everything going on." Jewel, please, you are going through, and it is just as important." "I think we should stay away from Crystal; we don't even know the story Cadence. This could be severe trouble we cannot afford.

....

Lakenya was nowhere to be found. It was assumed she was still in Chicago. She would not answer anyone's calls, her colleagues would not answer any questions, and even Bugsy was clueless. It had only been a week, but the threats from Crystal were more frequent, Cadence followed Jewel's advice and did not get into the confusion.

For the following six days, Hassan and the crew visited with Troy's mother to bring and eat a meal with her. She found slight comfort when she joined them in reliving moments of mischief; she often got them out of or punished them all for it. She would sit and stare at them and tell them how she saw her son in them all. They held her hands while also taking care of Tahiry that week. The fellas carried his casket, and they all sat with her and Crystal on the front row at his mother's request.

"I spoke to Lakenya this morning before the funeral. I didn't tell you all because I didn't want to get you upset." Troy's mother sat in the sunroom with her best friend, Tahiry's mother Dana, Crystal, Cadence, and her four friends. "I told her she is forgiven." "Mom?" Crystal interjected. "Hush, child!" spoken to her grown daughter. "Troy's father told me about the domestic violence that lived in their relationship." "What?" they all said simultaneously. "He sat me down last night and told me about some things he witnessed my son do to your friend. A lot of things I am ashamed to mention to you." Everyone sat wide-eyed and listened carefully. "Truth is, he learned that from my husband. When you all were younger." She looked to Crystal, "He'd beat me every day then take you for ice cream afterward. "When y'all got older, he'd wait until you weren't home. Those were the worst. The last time, I ended up in the hospital. He told me last night that Troy would watch every time. "Mommy!" Crystal fell to her mother's feet with tears in her eyes. "It's alright, baby." She rubbed her daughter's hair. "He gave his life to God and changed his ways. He was always a good father; it just took him a while to be a good husband." Tahiry's mother shook her head. "And this woman helped me through it all." She took her friend's hand and kissed it. "Lakenya was just protecting herself, and I forgive her, you must too." She looked to them all. Crystal sucked her teeth; Troy was her twin brother; she could care less about his abuse toward Lakenya. She felt Lakenya maybe deserved it, and she was not going to give up. News of her mother's damage was too much for her to bear. She stormed out of the sunroom without a word.

Everyone was speechless; they locked eyes with each other while gathering their thoughts. The silence went on until Troy's mother assured them all was well. The girls embraced her and cried for her. Troy's mother comforted them; she had no more tears left for herself. "I loved my son, and I know y'all did too. Y'all grew up like siblings, but he was not right. I don't think he was ever going to straighten out." She hung her head. "I told Lakenya she needs to come home for Tahiry. Y'all welcome her." She stood up and opened her arms for them to hug her.

"Let's call Kenya." Cadence suggested when they got to their cars in the packed yard. "where are you?" Jewell asked Lakenya. "In Chicago. Business is and always will be moving." She spoke as if she knew nothing. "What are you doing?" Jewel asked. "waiting for a client. He is treating me to lunch to wrap up some business." "Are you okay?" Cadence asked emphatically. "good as always." Lakenya replied quickly. "Troy's funeral was today. There was silence on the other end. "You haven't been home to see Tahiry." Cadence said innocently, "oh yeah, I heard she got shot in the throat and shoulder." Cadence put her hand over her friend's mouth to stop the cursing from coming. "How's mama James?" "not too well, she is worried sick," Cadence answered. "Damn the neck and shoulder, huh?" I wonder what her chances for survival are? Listen, I gotta go. I'm gonna catch a flight in a few days, but I'll call you back later tonight." Just like that, she was gone again.

Chapter 8

Regret

"I've been waiting for you, baby." Hassan sat at Tahiry's bedside with tears in his eyes. "We don't have to have babies, as long as you come back to me, I'll never ask anything of you." He whispered. "I was looking at the slide Cadence played at the dinner, and I realize we haven't taken a vacation in two years. You have to wake up so you can spend all my money babe, wake up. Wake up, baby." He wiped her hair from her face and shook her. "I need you, T, wake up!" he kissed her lips and began to cry. "I was so selfish; I'm so sorry, Tahiry." Hassan then just sat and wept. Once he pulled himself together, Hassan brought her up to speed on business as he always did and the fact that he left the turntable for good. And as usual, he did leg and arm exercises with her and played her favorite music. Throughout the day, doctors and nurses came and went, none came with good news, only thanks for the daily sweets his family had been sending to them. He put on a smile when necessary but was so torn inside. Seeing his childhood best friend and love of his life lying in bed, breathing with a machine was making him crazy.

In his mind, he replayed the last conversation they had and broke his own heart. The disrespectful way he threw other women in her face haunted him. He wondered at that moment how it had affected her. Hassan painfully remembered the look in her eyes when he called the wedding off, the torment he caused when he walked away without looking back. He recalled being so conflicted he could not remember what she looked like the last night he saw her alive. Of course, the pros in their relationship far outweighed the cons, smiling at each other seemed to be the only way they lived. Arguments were few and far between, and when there was an argument, it was more about leaving the toilet seat up, leaving empty boxes of cereal on the fridge, or the temperature in the house being too hot or cold. The disagreements were always minor. He briefly recalled listening to other friends complain about their non-cooking, greedy, cheating wives and realized how fortunate he was because he did not have one complaint. Tahiry worked and went to school full time, and still managed six home-cooked meals a week, kept a clean home, maintained his full loads of laundry, and took him on date nights. It was not until that moment did; he sincerely appreciates her.

"Hey, bruh." Cain stood in the doorway. "What's going on, brother?" Hassan asked solemnly. "Came to check sis out. Any improvement?" He eased closer to her bed. "Nah." Hassan grabbed her hand. "My baby is gonna leave me, bro." He blinked, and a tear rushed. "I shouldn't have left her alone, Cain. We've been inseparable since elementary school; I should not have left her alone." He sobbed with his head on her stomach. Cain put his hand on his friend's shoulder while he cried. Minutes later, Ahmad showed up to help comfort his brother. None of them had ever seen such grief.

Cadence and Jewel had a late lunch delivered for them. And with a few minutes to put their minds on something else, Cain became the object of a lengthy interrogation. "you just showed up, Cain. Where have you been?" Ahmad led the charge. "No bullshittin' either," Hassan added. "They sat close to the window overlooking the street, waiting for Cain's answer. "I was in Chicago with Lakenya." He said shamefully. "O fucking Kay." Said Ahmad. "some truth." Hassan let out a small laugh. "What are you thinking, dog?" "Cadence got a man now, right?" "Boy, that man ain't come around until after you disappeared." Hassan said. "you weren't with your baby's moms but with your lady's best friend?" "He never would leave that heifer alone. I'm surprised you never been caught." Ahmad chimed in. "I can remember a couple of times he almost did," Hassan said. "Where is she now? The girls are hot with her because she should be here." "I don't know." Cain shrugged. "She won't answer my calls, and she hasn't called either. "I don't know how I feel about seeing her," Ahmad growled. "I don't care what Troy's mom said, I do not forgive her." "what if what she said is true?" Hassan asked. "He did get pretty crazy, and we love Lakenya like a sister too, despite her whorish ways." Ahmad reluctantly shook his head in agreement, "Cadence better not find out about y'all two." Hassan pointed to Cain. "He is glad Frank isn't here because he doesn't play about Cadence. If he finds out you dogged her in this way, you may just have some trouble on your hands." Ahmad laughed. "Man, I'll fuck little buddy up." Cain said salty. "naaah, you will have trouble with that one." Hassan joined. "Well, Cady won't find out from me, but I can't speak for Lakenya; she's been reckless lately. "Y'all know she always was jealous of our ladies. Anything she could do to lessen what our girls did." Said Hassan. "Y'all remember when she cut her hair to look like Cadence's but ended up looking like the gay dude from low down dirty shame." The three of them laughed heartily. "She always comes up short." Said Ahmad, "except when it comes to you." Hassan pointed to Cain. "Even though y'all aren't together anymore, finding this news out would break her." "I doubt Lakenya will tell her. She is too invested in Cadence's and Jewel's protection from Crystal. She doesn't want to mess that up." Said Hassan. Cain stood up and walked closer to the window. "When Tahiry got shot. She called me before she left here to tell me not to answer your calls. She would not tell me what happened, and she sounded frantic. "What happened?" "Our engagement dinner ended early because she told me about Tahiry's abortion and the fact that it messed her up for good." He looked at Tahiry lying in bed, tubes stuck to her, and her chest was rising and falling with the sound of the machine. "I went home, Tahiry went her own way. An hour later, Cadence and Frankie just so happened to run upon the scene of the shooting on their way back to the hotel." "Was Lakenya at the hospital?" Cain asked. "Nah." Hassan replied, "Did she run up on the scene too?" "Nah, we all figured she was ashamed of herself and didn't think twice about her after that." Hassan shook his head. Cain replayed the details of his conversation with Lakenya when she told him about the shooting, but he kept those to himself.

"Who would want to shoot Tahiry?" The six of them sat in their favorite seafood spot for dinner. "We have no idea. Aside from that last fight in the club, Tahiry hasn't been into it with anyone." Said Cadence. She sat inside Frankie's arms exhausted from the prior week's events. "Of course, it wasn't her beef." Jewel interrupted Cadence's next statement. "It was Lakenya's." Jewel sat across from Ahmad and kept her eyes on her phone. "Which one of y'all told her about Tahiry?" Hassan asked. "Neither, we assumed Troy did." Their server appeared with their drinks. "Georgia Peach tea." He started with Cadence, "Three Bonnie and Clyde's," he served Jewel, Ahmad, and Hassan. "One smoke on the water," for Frankie, "and a big apple Manhattan" lastly for Cain. "He didn't," Ahmad answered Jewel. "He told me she wouldn't answer his calls." "We need to go see Bugsy's wife." Jewel announced. "we've been so wrapped in being at the hospital; we haven't wrapped our minds around figuring out who did this." "well, you won't be going alone," Hassan said. "Y'all are too emotional, and I don't trust you to remain calm." He finished his drink then pulled his cell out.

"Bugsy's wife had a history with them all. Bugsy never cared to involve himself with her troubles. He was cool with Hassan, Cain, and Ahmad and wanted it to stay that way. He waited for Bugsy to answer his phone call while everyone sat by. "What's up, San?" he answered. "I've meant to reach out after I heard about your lady. I'm sorry that happened to her." "Why?" Jewell blurted out; Ahmad put his hand over her mouth to stop her from talking. "Thanks, Bugs." "Even though I didn't fuck with him as I do you, Ahmad and Cain, I'm sorry about what happened to your boy too. Is it true he tried to rape Lakenya, though? He sounded sincere. "I don't know, man, that's just the story we got. But I am calling on behalf of the ladies." He needed not to call any names. "They want to talk to your wife." "About what?" he chuckled. "Tahiry's shooting." Hassan adjusted himself in his seat. "They wanna know if your wife or her girls were involved." Bugsy did not respond right away. They sat and waited while he gathered his thoughts. His offense was spoken through his silence. "Okay," he said slowly, "I'll set that up, but I can tell you they weren't. I know the ladies don't want to hear it from me, but their problems weren't with your lady or the other two, just Lakenya. I asked them about it when I heard the news." Bugsy went on. "They told me their hands were out of that. Meet us at my pool hall tomorrow around three." He hung up. "He sounded convincing," Cadence said before she dug into her lobster tail. "I'll still be seeing them tomorrow, though." Jewel would not let up.

"Tahiry was the one who knocked her out in that fight, and you know I don't trust Bugsy, he just doesn't want any problems." "that he doesn't," said Hassan. "I gotta thank you all for putting your lives on hold for T," Hassan raised his freshly refilled drink. "You too, Frankie, you didn't know my lady very well, but you've been here from the moment y'all saw the accident, and I am grateful for that." He sniffled. "I wouldn't have it any other way. I recognize the bond and respect yall have." Frankie replied. "You're our brother now, too," Ahmad announced and raised his glass regardless of Cain's feelings.

For the next hour, they enjoyed their steak and seafood over light conversation, and they took significant advantage of the bar so they could have the conversation they were dreading to have with one another, the possibility of Tahiry's death. The prospect of her coming out of the coma was unlikely, and none of them were trying to face it. Cadence and Jewel could not hold it together at the table. They cried as if they already received the news of her death; it was so heartbreaking, people from other tables were coming to console them. It was a moment none of them foresaw. They used the remainder of the night to discuss plans and their roles for their friend's funeral if it came to that.

....

"We appreciate you for setting this up, Bugs," Hassan said to Bugsy. He, his best friends, and best girls sat on one side of a table Bugsy put together for them. Bugsy, his wife Shana, and three of her friends sat with iced looks on the opposite side. "No problem, man, this is the least we could do," Bugsy replied. "A few months back, you ladies had a brawl with my ladies." Hassan looked into Shana's eyes and spoke slowly. "From what I was told, it didn't end well for you ladies; I only witnessed a small piece." He did not blink an eye; no one uttered a word. "A couple of weeks later, my lady ended up shot and left to die by herself on the side of the road." Hassan's breathing was shaky, Jewel and Cadence kept their composure and their eyes on Shana's friends who looked like they were ready to jump across the table. Silence filled the hall; smoke filled the air. Bugsy sat back and lit up while they hashed out their differences.

"Where's Lakenya?" Shana blurted with attitude. "She's where she should be," Jewel replied. She was the least happy with Lakenya but would not hesitate to protect her. "Always there to start trouble but never around for the fight." Shana laughed. "Just like when we were younger." She looked at her friends, and they laughed with her. Bugsy sat by with a smirk, his bloodshot eyes red. "Look," Shana sat up to the table, her friends adjusted themselves in their seats, Cadence and Jewel sat still. "we don't have a problem with you two or Tahiry. We are sorry about what happened to her, y'all always been cool until that girl starts shit. Yeah, Tahiry hit me, but I'd hit a bitch too if my best friend were a punk ass bitch." Jewell scowled "okay, that's enough. "You know we don't play that disrespectful shit." She waved her hand. "If we see her around during y'all time of caring or grief, we will stand down, but I will never get over the constant disrespect of her sleeping with my husband." Bugsy did not say a word; he simply smiled as if he got a kick out of his wife's statement. "We have nothing to do with that." Hassan interrupted. They all decided Lakenya would be fighting her own battles going forward, but the opposition would not be the first to know. "we just want to know if y'all had something to do with Tahiry being shot." Cadence spoke like she was talking to kindergartners.

She did not move a muscle, but she did not have to. Jewell was antsier, she leaned forward on the table to show she was ready for them. Patrons began to file in the hall slowly, a bartender popped out from the backroom and began prepping for the evening. "No!" Shana did not bat an eye. Her three friends sat with stupid, untrustworthy smiles on their faces. "That's all we needed." Hassan, Cadence and the fellas stood up; Jewel remained seated with her eyes on Shana, then her friends next to her.

Lakenya's number was immediately dialed the second they stepped out of Bugsy's place. To their surprise, she answered on the first ring. She sounded happy. "You need to come home." Jewel did not waste time with pleasantries. "Well, what's going on? Is it Tahiry? My lawyer says I should stay away for a while until…you know." She hushed someone in the background. "Well, you know nothing is happening when you are with us." Jewell laid it on thick. "Crystal is cool; Shana has agreed to chill too." She went on. "What does Shana have to do with this?" Kenya asked. "We stopped by to make sure there wasn't any static with her concerning Tahiry's shooting." Lakenya went silent. "Hello?" "I'm here, Jewel. I'll get a flight out at the end of the week." "End of the week?" Cadence asked Hassan, and the fellas looked with surprise. "Yeah, I'm in the middle of a big closing, and it's taking longer than usual." "We could give a fu…...." "Just get here soon as you can," Cadence interrupted Jewel. Silence once again, "okay, I will fly out tomorrow, let me get some things together. I'll be bringing someone with me too, so don't be trippin'." She hung up without another word.

·········

"What big closing? Do you need help? Asked Rascheen. "oh none. I was just buying myself a few days." "Why are you avoiding going home? He asked, "well, you know, the shooting." She plopped on the white couch she forbade anyone to sit on. "But it's so much more than that." She hesitated. The secret that festered inside wanted to break only for someone she trusted. Rascheen kept talking, but she could not hear him. Out of nowhere, a pouring rain hid the scenery she had fixated on outside her large window. Rascheen finally caught on that she was not listening, he sat next to her on the couch and shook her. I'll book us a flight; it's going to be okay." He assured her. "Do it for Wednesday. I need another day to gather my thoughts. And how do you know things will be fine?" she stood up to a bottle of vodka. "My friends hate me right now for telling Tahiry's secret. Hassan probably has a hit out on me now." She took two shots quickly. "He's been at her side since we were kids." She lit a cigarette. "He was so disgusted; he left the dinner before any of us." She recalled. "You are going to have to face them soon Lakenya, they are your friends, and they need you." Maurice did not know how misleading his words were. "I'm ready to meet them." Rascheen's naïve smile got on her nerves. "What are you going to tell your wife?" "Ah, I'll just drop a few dollars on her and the kids, she'll never know I'm gone." "What did I tell you about giving her money?" Lakenya snapped and smirked. "That'll be the only time she releases me without trouble." "yeah, AND when it's time for sex." She poured another shot. "That's why I am here." He looked to her with a greedy smile. "She doesn't drive me the way you do." He sat next to her. "Drive you to do what?" she rolled her eyes. "To be completely myself in the bedroom and out of it too. She's so stuck up and, you are as loose as they come." She did not take that as a compliment. "I just mean I can be myself with you. I love you, Lakenya." She laughed, "You don't love me, you love the way I lick your ass. Go to the store for cigars; I need to smoke some weed." "That too!" Rascheen said before he jumped to do what he was told.

"I'll be in South Carolina the day after tomorrow; I'll have someone with me but don't trip because he is going to be around a lot when y'all come back to Chicago." She watched Rascheen back out of her driveway. "I need a favor." She slowly walked the wide hallway to her bedroom. "Bugsy's wife, Shana…. She's been issuing threats to me, and she needs to be out of my way when I get there." She pulled the gun she used on Troy from her closet.

"See, that's why I love you. You make sure I am taken care of in all ways." She licked her lips. "I want to look in her eyes first." She laughed. "Who have you been giving my dicks too?" she asked with attitude. "Well, when I'm home, you know what time it is. I gotta go." She hung up. Lakenya's devious smile displayed over her face as she thought of the savage young boys who satisfied her in their way. A great addition to her collection, the boys had ten times the thug quality Troy had but without the hassle.

"Cain!" she immediately dialed his number. "Why haven't I heard from you?" She played as if she had not seen him calling for the past couple of weeks. "I miss you." She said sweetly, whatever his response was brought a huge smile to her face. "I'll be home Thursday; I can't wait to see you." She paused for him to speak. "Yeah, yeah, I know we can't be seen together, I'll have someone with me anyway…. How you know?" She had no idea he was listening in on the call with the girls. "I need you to find some time for me, though." Regardless of the gang of children Cain had at home, Lakenya spoke intending to bring him back to Chicago also. She loved making messes for herself. Cain did not need to know the mess Lakenya had planned for Shana. She kept quiet about it and told him she would be there a day later than she would be. Not once did Lakenya ask about Tahiry or the others, she made it clear they were not her concern. She picked his brain for whatever information he had about any suspects and cut him off when he went off the subject. Lakenya filled Cain's head with the freaky things she had planned for him the day after she arrived.

In her go-bag, she threw the usual toiletries, a small bag of cocaine, her other cell phone, an I pad and some cash. She tightly wrapped her gun and placed it in a box for the delivery service. The fear of facing her friends sent a tremble through her. Thoughts of good days where they were happy with one another, shopping, vacationing, partying, cruising, and living life brought a slight smile to her face. Lakenya then looked around and admired her Bentley home collection, the paintings from collectors she sought hard to find, and the kitchen that belonged in a magazine and appreciated the way Cadence's exceptional taste rubbed off on her. A little tour she took herself on led her to the fifth bedroom she used as her home office. Along the walls, she had painted gold were awards, plaques, certifications, degrees, and medals she had earned since high school. Jewel was Lakenya's educational motivator. She often did Lakenya's work resulting in a lot of the accolades she was so proud of on that wall. Next door was the bedroom that put her in mind of them all. Cadence chose the white jeweled king bed; the Italian made mirrored armoire, antiqued mirror chest, and the sheepskin bench with stiletto legs. Above the bed was a framed copy of the six-figure check that Jewel always told her she would get. Her walk-in closet was filled with clothes inspired by Tahiry. She was aware her style could not touch Tahiry's on a tough day, but she tried. Each of them had a hand in building in Lakenya what came naturally to them. Two pairs of sneakers and three stilettos were thrown in Lakenya's shoe bag. She pulled two black dresses, three jumpsuits, two Nike tracksuits, one Jordan sweatsuit, and a trench dress from luggage, along with the jewelry box that held her platinum accessories.

"Kenya!" Rascheen called from the door; she met him in the hallway with her luggage in tow. "I got you some Korean barbecue." Her cell had a text alert. "Yes," she thought to herself. "Finally, the dick pics I asked Cain for." "Thanks, Scheen. Would you roll a couple for me please?" she wheeled her bags to their bedroom and set them in the doorway. "These next few days are going to be hectic. "she led Maurice to her den, plopped on her the couch again, then responded to the text. "would you put my food in the kitchen please.?" She did not take her eyes off the phone. "is there anything I need to know before we get there?" he asked when he returned. He lit the tightly rolled blunt and passed it off. "Just that they will be a little off-putting when they see you. Do not wear your wedding ring, that's additional questions." Rascheen laughed.

Chapter 9

The Hardest Part

"The kids have been fed, I've given them their baths, and they are almost asleep. You should just let them stay." Jewel's mother in law said sweetly. "It's Friday, you had a busy week, and they will be fine. Go home and relax." Jewel did not hesitate to turn her car around and head to her house. Usually, she would be excited to go home to her husband and a quiet evening at home, but since he had been at a hotel for a few weeks, she thought about her empty house and the cold bottle of wine in her fridge.

She took a slight detour to the Chinese restaurant close to her house. From the parking lot, she called in her order for a sweet and sour chicken dinner and watched the customers pour in and out of the small restaurants. The two young ladies at the counters reminded her of Tahiry and herself when they were in high school working for the same Chinese spot. She giggled at one of them, storing her number in a cute customer's phone. Back in their day, they had to write their numbers down on receipt paper. Ahmad and Hassan would find out and scare them all away, young men and grown ones alike. She took the rest of the time to scroll on her Facebook page. After laughing at the many pictures that so accurately and hilariously described a typical black household, she came across a R.I.P post. Someone had taken one of Shana's images from her Facebook page and photoshopped some wings on her. The caption read "fly high baby girl," and it included her sunrise and sunset dates. Jewell was speechless. She kept scrolling and read the numerous posts about the shock of Shana's death. More posts were aimed toward her killers; there were threats of finding them and doing them worse than what was done to her. Earlier she scrolled past a picture of a man she knew from her old neighborhood, she liked it and kept going. It was not until she saw Donte and Shana's pictures side by side did Jewel put together that Donte had been killed too. More posts about Donte began to flood her timeline. The mother of his children posted her outrage about the killers and the fact that Shana was with him when he died. There were rumors about the two of them messing around; now everyone knew it was true.

"Damn!" Jewell said to herself when she got back in her car. In less than five minutes, Jewell was pulling in her yard. The sun began to set behind her home slowly, and it gave off one single ray that highlighted the person standing in her bright green grass. For a moment, it looked like Tahiry dressed in white. Her brown skin shined underneath her full golden afro. Jewell immediately halted when she realized it was Cadence. No words were needed; the solemn look and dried tears on Cadence's face said it all. Jewell ran to embrace her friend so they could cry together. They could not let go until Frankie pulled in the yard with Hassan in the passenger seat and Ahmad in the back.

"We have to go." Cadence sniffled. "Mama J's giving us time to see her before she goes to the morgue, but we don't have long. She let Jewel get in the back first so she could lean on Ahmad. He immediately grabbed her hand. Hassan sat in front, no emotions in his eyes as he swayed with the movements of the truck. The radio was off, but their faint whimpers and sniffles filled the air.

"Do you need to be alone, Hassan?" Cadence asked. The six of them stood at the room door, hesitant to go inside. "No, I need y'all." He said. "we need each other." Jewell followed. Hassan touched the doorknob then drew his hand back. Both Ahmad and Cain put their hands on his shoulders, letting him know to take his time. They could feel the hospital staff watching them with sorrow. Hassan finally opened the door to the cold, quiet hospital room. "Oh, Tahiry!" Cadence led the grief parade. Frankie and Cain leaped to her side, Hassan and Ahmad stuck close to Jewel. The ladies held her cold hands and kissed her freezing forehead. The men could not control themselves; the moment Hassan had the chance to grieve, they would not let him cry alone.

"Is she dead?" Lakenya asked from the doorway. Jewel wiped her eyes then charged her way. "The hell you wanna know for? Where have you been all this time?" She could only scream because of Hassan and Ahmad holding her back. Everyone else looked on. Cadence usually tried to stop Jewel from going to Lakenya's head, but she looked as if she agreed. "She just passed an hour ago, Kenya." Cain pushed passed Ahmad and Hassan, settling Jewel down. Before she spoke again, it was apparent that she was trying to force some tears. "I'm so sorry," she finally let out. "What took you so long to get here?" he asked. "The weather messed up my flight plans." She said with ease while trying to peek around Cain. "You're going to need to give the girls some time. They will probably call you when we leave here." He closed the door in her face. Lakenya was embarrassed in front of the same staff she just got loud with before she opened the room door.

"Now comes the hard part," Cadence said after they piled back in Frankie's Mercedes truck. "I suggest we put our phones on, do not disturb, and stay away from social media for a couple of days." "Hassan, you should come and stay with Ahmad and me," Jewell suggested. He did not answer, but he knew he would. They rode quietly back to Jewel's house, finding her car door open the way she left it. Her keys were still in the ignition. Cain tried to bring up Lakenya's appearance, but none of them wanted to hear it. They unanimously decided to put her off for a couple of days too.

Mama J's house was full of her family. Troy's mother was in the kitchen, cooking and arranging food and drinks as they were brought in. Tahiry's first cousins had formed a shield around mama J, who sat lifeless in her living room. Children ran in and out of the front and back doors of the house. Outside were more cousins leaning against their cars, smoking and laughing loudly, and uncles firing up their grills. It was twenty-four hours after Tahiry passed, and the six of them were just going through the motions. They sat in the living room with Mama J speaking when they were introduced and laughing at the occasional joke. In the back of their minds lingered the same thoughts. If Tahiry had her way, she would prefer the gathering be at Cadence or Jewel's house. Her relationship was forever estranged with her mother; she would only participate in the wedding activities because of Cadence's insistence. The cousins who flocked close couldn't come up with a memory, Tahiry's mother didn't know she was going to receive her Ph.D., and the family that was close to Tahiry and knew her well were forbidden to come because it was her father's family.

Cadence took all she could stand before she respectfully asked to help with the arrangements and let her know that she would host a gathering for close friends at her home. She knew Mama J would be happy. She had no idea how she would pay for a funeral. They gladly left her home, relieved they would not have to go back for a while.

In her home office, Cadence sat behind her cherrywood desk, penning a poem for Tahiry's obituary. Jewel lounged on the loveseat of the bonded leather Y shaped sofa, thinking of the perfect song for her solo. A knock on the door grabbed their attention and took it off the sorrowful occasion. The distraction was not much help; it was Lakenya, ready to talk it out. Jewel immediately moved to take a seat in the chairs across from Cadence's desk. "Have a seat Kenya; we don't have much time," Cadence spoke as if she was talking to an employee. She sat back in her stressless magic chair. Jewel sat quietly with her eyes straight forward; the disgust was displayed all over her face. Cadence was expecting an apology without any idea how upset she should have been.

Lakenya took her time getting to her chair, looking around because she has never been there before. "What's the word on the funeral?" she sat slowly. Cadence turned around and looked at the clock on the wall behind her. "In thirty minutes, Tahiry's people will be walking through my doors." She said in a low tone. "The next words that come out of your mouth better be the right ones or Jewel, and I will drag your broken body before them. Jewel finally looked Lakenya's way. Cadence's ice-cold stare frightened her. "I know you are all angry with me," Kenya said calmly. "You have every right to be. I am so sorry." "She hung her head for show. "For what exactly?" Jewel asked. "For ruining Tahiry's engagement? For not being here all those weeks, she laid up in the hospital? For being a terrible friend?" Jewel asked.

"And for being selfish," Lakenya stated and remained calm, she knew Cadence and Jewel would make good on their threat. "I got caught up with work, and Troy's shooting almost made me insane." She knew that would tug at their heartstrings, so she saved it for last. "and abuse Lakenya." Cadence fell for it. "All those years, you couldn't tell us that man was putting his hands on you." "Later for that!" Jewel did not bite. She stared into Lakenya's face with plenty of doubt in hers. "Our sister is gone; we do not want you here if you're going to start trouble." She stood up and put her index finger in the air, "we do not want you here if you intend on making one second about you." She held up her middle finger and turned it around to face Lakenya. She took a step closer to her old friend and held the third finger up. "we will not clean any of your messes. From the moment you stepped your black ass on that plane to Chicago, you forfeited any right to help from me." She took one more step, so the tip of her nose would kiss Lakenya's, "If you plan on sticking around, keep your mouth closed. Don't make me check you." Jewell stared into Lakenya's eyes for minutes without blinking then turned to walk away. "She's finished with you." Cadence Shrugged.

Chapter 10

Saying Goodbye

"So, I guess you will introduce me at the wake?" Rascheen sat and watched Lakenya squeeze into one of the dresses from her bag. "Yes, just relax, I will." "You've been strange since we got here. I have seen this city on my own in an uber. You brought me, and you dropped me." He stepped behind her, kissed her shoulders before she slid the dress over them, and he helped her zip up. "I apologize. Some unexpected things came up." She moved to the mirror to position her new lace front correctly. "The wake is in an hour; then we are going to Cadence's. "She turned around and threw her arms around his neck. "You're gonna meet everyone, and they are gonna love you." She kissed him sweetly to calm his nerves. "So, you wanna tell me what's up?" he leaned in the doorway. Her quietness was nothing like the Lakenya he knew. "Nothing." She brushed the question off. "Is that what you are wearing?" Rascheen looked down at his red Ferragamo slippers, black slacks, dress tee, and his floral print Tom Ford blazer. "Yes." He said firmly. Criticizing his attire was the way to back him off even though he was dressed very nicely.

Tahiry's death still had not reached her brain, everything else came first, Troy, Shana, her two little boos, Rascheen and even Cain. There was a knock on their room door before Rascheen called her name. Cadence stood in front of the door in her green trench coat, yellow heels, and olive tinted sunglasses. "Just thought I would drop by to remind you to stay on your good behavior and use your inside voice at all times." Cadence removed her shades and invited herself inside. Lakenya was kind of heated after she spoke without a hello. "Who is this?" "Rascheen, this is Cadence, he is a friend." She responded to Cadence's question. "okay, it's nice to meet you. I've heard a lot about you." he extended his hand. Cadence hesitated but shook. "I'm sure." Cadence said dryly. "umm, can I have a moment alone with Lakenya, please?" she pointed to Lakenya. Rascheen went into the adjoining part of the suite. Cadence paced the floor until she heard the door close. Her demeanor was icy. "SOOO, I'm busy planning the funeral of my best friend, and my phone is blowing up." She began. "Do you remember Lewis from Lincoln Apartments?" Lakenya nodded slowly. "Somehow, he got my number to interrupt my business to discuss you." She continued to pace. "Word is, you have been hanging around Corey and Lawrence a lot lately. Word is also that you were with them when they killed Shana and Donte." She stopped and stared at Lakenya. She did not know how to respond, so she did not. She immediately thought about putting her boys on a plane. "Now, what do you think will happen when Bugsy finds this news out?" She began to pace again after Lakenya would not respond. Lakenya was frightened. She knew precisely what Bugsy was capable of. She hardly handled the fights that she was protected from over the years. She saw the worry on Cadence's face, small bags under her brown eyes. "If he or Lewis or anyone from their camp comes anywhere near us, I will point them in your direction."

"So, that's our friendship now?" Lakenya finally spoke. "Lakenya, when was the last time you saw Xavier?" Cadence asked about Lakenya's sixteen-year-old son. "When I fucked his father last month." She said coldly. "I pay my child support." Cadence shook her head. "It's better that way." "Now, you know we are better than that." Cadence scolded. "Where are your children, Cadence?" She asked smartly. Cadence only chuckled and smiled. "I won't dignify that stupidity with an answer. However, I will say, do not push me because you know I will take it there." Cadence kept eye contact. Lakenya's ears burned at the sound of Cadence's threat. Her devil knelt on her left shoulder and whispered for Lakenya to get her gun. The devil inside her cracked a smile with intention. "I hope you hear me, Lakenya." Cadence continued. "We will not tolerate any drama near Tahiry's wake, her funeral, the burial, or my house. Jewel does not know about the call I got or this little meeting, and if you act right, she will not. She's already angry." Cadence gave Lakenya a chance to speak before she turned to walk away.

It was as if the funeral already happened. Cadence's living room, sunroom, entertaining room, and her backyard was full of mourners. Everyone there had been a part of the private viewing Cadence planned for immediate family, and a shortlist of close friends. It was quiet. The busy passing by of vehicles on Cadence's street could be heard inside. Seeing Tahiry lifeless in her eternal bed was a shock to them all, even though they knew better, she looked like she was sleeping peacefully after a facial that made her skin glow. The platinum tiara with pink diamonds fit perfectly around her head, draped with her natural curls. She was beautiful, even in death.

Cadence was too exhausted after the day's events, so she went straight to her bedroom. After changing into sweats, t-shirts, and jeans, everyone else lounged around while the guests mixed around. Words were not needed; their feelings were worn on their faces. Jewel was snuggled under Ahmad on the loveseat, Frankie and Cadence sat together on the sectional and Lakenya was fitted on Rascheen's lap by the bar. The door swung open, in rushed Cain. "We've got company, but the fellas need to handle it. Lakenya, you need to get out of sight." He nodded his head in the direction of the men to follow.

Cadence could not rest, a hot shower, a hot cup of tea, and a joint Jewel left in her nightstand could not calm her. While everyone was in her home and backyard, forcing themselves to have a good time, Cadence struggled to get the rest she so desperately needed. Trying to watch tv only reminded her of the tragedy, the local news reported no leads in Tahiry's murder investigation. Underneath the sixty-inch flatscreen tv on her berry painted wall, Tahiry's life was summarized in a beautiful gold box on Cadence's dresser. Mama J's name flashed across her cell's screen; she ignored it, knowing she was calling for more money. Life had become the more hectic when Cadence was given full reigns over Tahiry's funeral arrangements. She just laid and stared at the box until her presence was requested in her living room. With no desire to keep up appearances, she threw her pink silk robe over her braless tank top and boy shorts. Pink socks rode her thick thighs, and the silk bonnet matched them. "We have some unexpected company," Jewel whispered to Cadence. She snuck away to tell Cadence after she was told to stay put.

It was Bugsy, with a look that would kill on his face. He stood alone; he never had anyone close enough to ride with or for him. Hassan backed the rest of the men off before he took Bugsy into Cadence's office. "What's going on?" Jewel whispered with attitude to Cadence. She knew something was not right. Cadence could not tell her; she knew Lakenya would have been walked out to the plank by Jewel herself. Instead of answering Jewel, Cadence quietly went to her office behind the men. Bugsy explained his presence as respectfully as possible. He fought through his words with gasps and small weeps but let Hassan know that he was certain Lakenya was involved with the death of his wife, and he wanted her dead in revenge. He went on to explain how his respect was wearing thin for them, especially if they knew about Lakenya's involvement. His retaliation was that moment; he asked for Hassan to bring Lakenya to him so he could take her away. He was no longer considering the mourning taking place at Cadence's house.

In front of the door, Cadence stood, scared out of her mind. Bugsy was a badass, that is why he could travel alone. She did not know whether to call the police or shoot him in the back. She figured that would be the time she should utilize the skills she acquired from the target practice and weapons permit Cain pushed her to get. Hassan lied about Lakenya being there. Bugsy allowed Hassan to tell him about the differences between the girls and how they had practically shunned her from the crew. It was a distraction, of course, Cadence spoke up when she heard them talking about the girls, and startled them a bit. Hassan scolded her for what she was wearing but backed up her story. They both told Bugsy that they knew Lakenya was in town, and they would for sure see her again. Hassan assured Bugsy that he knew his pain, but he warned him against catching Cadence, or Jewel up in anything he planned to do to Lakenya.

......

Pink bouquets, a beautiful pink casket spread, and white roses were draped over the custom pink casket with Tahiry's name engraved at the bottom. She did not belong to a church, but it was essential to everyone that she would be funeralized in one. It was a dark day, typical South Carolina winter weather. The wind was slight and mellow to the senses. One by one, Cadence and her friends piled into the Mercedes family car that was to take them to meet mama. J's car, and most of the processional when they arrived in Charleston. They merged into the funeral line at meeting street; the second car stopped as instructed to let them in. Less than a mile away, they slowly rode to their destination in silence.

Grace cathedral, seated in the Charleston historic district, was the perfect place to memorialize her friend. They visited once to attend the christening of Tahiry's colleague's child, and they fell in love with the architectural beauty of the place. Inside the sanctuary, friends, colleagues, and acquaintances filled the pews. A fast rendition of precious lord played by a hired musician echoed throughout the place. Once assembled in order of mama J's approval, the doors opened, the pastor ordered the congregation to stand. Mama J, Hassan, Cadence, Jewel, Ahmad, and Cain led the line. Mama J's sisters and their children were next and followed by their cousins. Almost everyone was dressed in black with a pink flower or ribbon that was given at the door. Cadence and Jewel wore matching light pink blouses with black pencil skirts. Hassan and the men wore pink shirts under their jackets.

The pews were long enough to fit them all on the first row. As everyone came in behind them and filled in the seat, Cadence took Hassan and Jewel's hand; Jewel grabbed Ahmad. All their eyes were on the coffin, still in front of them. It held an important piece of them for over twenty years. Pastor Briggs, a personal friend of mama J's, stood before the large congregation with a welcoming spirit. He made it clear he intended to celebrate Tahiry and worship God during it all. The religious folks in the building raised a scattered amount of amens and hallelujahs. Briggs began with the standard funeral scripture Psalm 23. He added at the end how he hoped she let the lord lead her to the path of righteousness while she walked this earth so that she would live in God's house. He read from the book of Isaiah to comfort the family; in his words, "Those who call on God will find the strength they did not know they had." None of it resonated with Tahiry's friends; they only focused on the box that sat still in front of them. Cadence and Jewel hid behind their black sunglasses and blotted tears away. The singing from the combined church choir, the testaments from the many people who came in contact with, and loved her dearly, and finally, the preaching of the eulogy was a blur to everyone who sat on the first pew. It was only when the funeral servicemen opened the casket did, they come back with the rest of the church. Immediately, their grief spilled in front of everyone. The parade of people viewing Tahiry was a who's who of the community the girls grew up in. Old classmates, new friends, colleagues, hood superstars, community leaders, and students all showed up to pay their respect.

Lakenya was the first of the pew to visit the casket. Rascheen followed close behind with his hand on the small of her back. She stood over Tahiry without any emotion. Lakenya did not try to pretend to grieve over her friend. Cadence and Jewel watched with disgust, but mama J insisted she'd be there. Despite being told what to wear, she showed in a green dress that was too short and too tight. Ahmad held Jewell from getting out of her seat after she threatened to remove Lakenya from the church. For the final few seconds of her performance mourn, Lakenya lifted her sunglasses to wipe an imaginary tear then stumbled back so Rascheen would have to carry her away.

Cain was next, tears were already streaming as he approached. Those who could not see him felt his pain through his reaching cries. He took his time to say goodbye to his little sister. He stroked her arm and said I love you many times before the crew joined him to support. Instead of taking her seat with everyone else, Jewel stayed at the altar with Ahmad at her side. She stood and sighed for a second. She smiled and whispered, then broke down and cried. Ahmad was strong; he let his emotions run the day before at her viewing, so he held her while she rocked in his arms. Most of her cries were masked by the second up-tempo selection the choir prepared, they sang their hearts out but kept their eyes on the scene like everyone else. Once again, the rest of the crew except Lakenya and Rascheen came up for support. Jewel's cries seemed endless, but no one cared, most of the people in the church knew their back story.

Cadence's alone time was slightly different at first. She put her head on her friend's chest and said a few words. When she came up to glance for one last time, she cried like a baby. Frankie was there to hold her; she lost her knees when she said the words goodbye, and I love you. She sobbed the hardest and the longest. The crew gave her time to grieve before they joined her. Their presence soothed her much; she sighed heavily and stood for just a few more minutes before turning to walk away.

Hassan stopped her and the rest; he wanted them all to say one last goodbye together, and he knew he needed the support. His best friends minus one, stood behind him while he wept. Hassan's show of sorrow changed everyone's mind about men and their emotions. It was the saddest sight to see as he called her name and moaned he was sorry until his voice went hoarse. He bent down for one last kiss goodbye then had to be pulled away.

Hassan, Ahmad, and Cain accompanied mama J. Her boyfriend came to her side from the visitor pews. The congregation became restless; their whispers of conversation became loud and forceful. Mama J just ignored and rubbed her daughter's head. She took less time and was way less dramatic with her visit.

Hassan and everyone stood around mama J while she, Cadence, and Jewel put the veil over Tahiry's beautiful, restful face.

The worse day of their lives was almost over. Most of the congregants were gone once they viewed Tahiry; the handful that was left was shown out by the ushers. Each of them knew the burial would probably be the hardest for Hassan and wished they did not have to endure it. An almost truth to their wish when they finally made it outside behind the pallbearers. Waiting to follow the funeral cars to the burial site was the rest of the congregation from the church, but so much more was waiting on the family as well.

What seemed like the entire police and sheriff departments were blocking any exit out of the parking lot. The sun had made an appearance, as did everyone who followed the family out of the church. The wind had not stopped, nor had the temperature risen. As many people were outside and the number of cars passing by, the atmosphere was too quiet. The funeral servicemen continued their jobs as if nothing were happening. Slowly, whispers began when the suited down officer approached Lakenya with a look of steel on her face. "Lakenya Martin?" she asked with tenacity. "I need you to come with me…"

EPILOGUE

One dim flood light hung from the ceiling. There was a faint sound of water dripping, but there were no pipes or sinks around. Lakenya tapped her lime green nails on the rocky table underneath her elbows. It had been an hour since she had been pulled away from Tahiry's funeral and left alone in a cold medium lit room in the police station. Her mind was racing but she knew she was being watched. She kept a a cool face but her knee jerked wildly under the table.

"Ms. Martin." The detective waltzed in the room with a few large brown envelopes tucked under her arm. "I have to say, I was quite surprised when I was sent to pick you up. "Do I know you?", Lakenya asked with an attitude. She turned around to look at the second detective standing quietly at the door. "Well you should." She pulled up a seat. "My husband and I bought a house from you when I made lead detective a year ago." "Oh." Lakenya said lifelessly. "We also refered you to a few friends and I heard you did very well. Congrats on the top agent in the state award." She said facetiously. Lakenya did not reply.

"Well I am detective walker." She said with jurisdiction. "And I have been investigating the murders of Mrs. Shana Stevens, A Mr. Donte Scott." Dectective Walker fumbled through her paperwork. "Oh! And your friend, Tahiry James." She slid a picture of Tahiry across the table. "Who would have guessed you run with thugs." The detective pulled Tahirys photo away and replaced them with photos of her dread head and tatooed play things. "Lawrence Ulmer and Cory McFadden." The detective stated and sat back in the chair. "We were looking for them at the funeral

today. "Lakenya still would not speak.

"I don't think she understands that this is a two way conversation." The second detective startled Lakenya with his outburst from behind her. "Oh okay." Detective Walker chuckled. "Well listen to this." She sat up and spoke sarcastically with her hands folded on the table. "We have evidence. It's either them or you." "Plain!" said the second detective. "Someone is going down for these murders, framed or not." She smiled greedily. Lakenya looked around at the stone walls then the two detectives with the anxious looks. She was not sure if the water had stopped or the voices of the two detectives was drowning the sound. She could only imagine what the rest of the place looked like and was not willing to find out. She leaned over the desk and asked, "What do you want to know?

....

The sunrise over the clear blue water on the beach mesmerized Hassan. He stood shirtless with his arms above his head and rested on the doorway to the deck. He breahted in through his nose and exhaled hard as his mind ran across Tahiry. Cocoa Island in the Maldives would have awed her.

Steady breaths came in between the steps he took to reach his favorite lounge chair for the last week. It was paradise; the villa that stood over water brought such a calm to him. He slid into the lounge chair with ease and closed his eyes immediately. It had been too long since he had a moment to himself. Cadence and Jewell came the more overprotective of Hassan since Tahiry's death. Whie he appreciated the meals, the help around the house and his shops, he needed space more than anything.

As usual, Tahiry's face appeared when he closed his eyes and he smiled. Only her face, her hair was blacked out, no make up was used to hide her flawless skin and her smile was as bright as ever. No doubt it was the sun warming his body but he felt like it was in time with Tahiry's beam. A cold sensation against his arm made him snap his eyes open.

"You have the most beautiful smile baby." He was passed a cold beer and his lips were met with the taste of sweet cherries. "Thank you." Hassan dimmed his smile before he popped the top on the can. He stayed silent so he would not give off his frustration of his memory being interrupted. The subtle fresh breeze pushed his back against the cushioned vinyl lounge; this time he kept his eyes fixed on the umbrella above his eyes. "It's so quiet here." His vacation guest complained. "I had so much more fun in California baby." Hassan rolled his eyes and shook his head. His experience was not the same. In and out of expensive boutiques and shoe stores during the day; long nights in clubs he shyed from had him exhausted. Just when his mind said to let her go when they got back to South Carolina, she grabbed his hand and said, "I'm pregnant."

....

"Well have you seen him yet?" Jewel looked through the window nervously. She bit her lip each time she saw a car pass by. "Would you relax Jewelly." Cadence pulled her friend away. "You are starting to sweat." She blotted her friend's forehead. "You are going to mess up your make up and CeCe is going to have a fit." They laughed together. "I miss Tahiry." Jewel looked down. " I low key miss Lakenya too. I wish we could go back to the sixth grade. " I don't know about all that but I miss Kenya a little too. Tahiry's birthday is right around the corner." Cadence whispered. "It's the first one, and almost a year since she was killed." Jewel sniffled. "We should throw a huge party and maybe invite Lakenya." Jewel rolled her eyes. "Don't take it too far now." They laughed. "I'm going to see if I see your husband.

Just as Cadence left the room; Jewel's aunt Deborah flung the door open. She stood in the doorway with both hands on her face. "We were not going to start without you." Jewel smile. "Auntie DeDe!" Cadence ran for a hug. Deborah was speechless when she turned around to get a good look at her niece. "Oh stop it auntie. You have seen me like this before." Jewel spun in the white pearl

embelished mermaid wedding dress tailored for her body. "You are glowing baby girl. Well, I saw Cain, Hassan and Frankie, but where is Ahmad?" Deborah asked. "Who knows." CeCe butted into the conversation. The outside chaos of a panicked wedding party began to spill into the quiet place. "The flower girl does not have flowers!" the coordinator shouted. "Tracy!" someone called for the coordinator. "Gabby left her shoes at the hotel." Gabby was a bridesmaid, the hotel was twenty minutes away. "Okay! Everybody out!" Cadence commanded "The reason the bride is in this room is so she would not be exposed to that! Work it out people but do it OUT THERE!" She rushed them out.

"You and Ahmad have been through the hardest trials. " Said Cadence when the noise left the room and she took a seat next to the bride. "Remember we used to say how we wanted a marriage just like yours?" "Yeah." Jewel chuckled. "Y'all were crazy." She shook her head. " A lot of those trials, you went through alone. You put on a pretty face and went along like it was nothing." Jewel hung her head. "Promise me this time will be different." Cadence lifted Jewel's head by the chin. "Oh absolutely!" Jewel smiled. "Demetrius and I are a perfect pair." Jewel looked into the mirror. "That you are." Cadence stood to her feet. "I have to tell you something." She paced to the door to make sure it was locked. "I'm pregnant." Cadence said with regret. "It's Hassan's."

www.ingramcontent.com/pod-product-compliance
Lightning Source LLC
Chambersburg PA
CBHW031443130726
47989CB00003B/1269